"Toes Warm Enough Now?"

Pete asked.

Smiling, Abby angled her head back. "I'm warm all over."

She hadn't intended the double entendre, but of course the hidden meaning jumped out at her the moment the words were out. A glint appeared in Pete's indigo eyes.

"Me, too," he admitted. "All over."

Abby's pulse tripped, skipped, then took off at triple speed. She might not have meant to convey a sensual message in her comment, but Pete certainly did.

"Abby?" he asked in a husky voice.

"Mmm?"

"About that kiss at the airport?"

"Yes?"

"I told you I wasn't sorry. But if I kiss you again, I'm afraid I might be. Because a kiss won't be enough this time."

Dear Reader,

The holidays are always a busy time of year, and this year is no exception! Our "banquet table" is chock-full of delectable stories by some of your favorite authors.

November is a time to come home again—and come back to the miniseries you love. Dixie Browning continues her TALL, DARK AND HANDSOME series with *Stryker's Wife*, which is Dixie's 60th book! This MAN OF THE MONTH is a reluctant bachelor you won't be able to resist! Fall in love with a footloose cowboy in *Cowboy Pride,* book five of Anne McAllister's CODE OF THE WEST series. Be enthralled by *Abbie and the Cowboy*—the conclusion to the THREE WEDDINGS AND A GIFT miniseries by Cathie Linz.

And what would the season be without HOLIDAY HONEYMOONS? You won't want to miss the second book in this cross-line continuity series by reader favorites Merline Lovelace and Carole Buck. This month, it's a delightful wedding mix-up with *Wrong Bride, Right Groom* by Merline Lovelace.

And that's not all! *In Roared Flint* is a secret baby tale by RITA Award winner Jan Hudson. And Pamela Ingrahm has created an adorable opposites-attract story in *The Bride Wore Tie-Dye.*

So, grab a book and give *yourself* a treat in the middle of all the holiday rushing. You'll be glad you did.

Happy reading!

Lucia Macro

Senior Editor
and the editors of Silhouette Desire

Please address questions and book requests to:
Silhouette Reader Service
U.S.: 3010 Walden Ave., P.O. Box 1325, Buffalo, NY 14269
Canadian: P.O. Box 609, Fort Erie, Ont. L2A 5X3

MERLINE
LOVELACE
WRONG BRIDE, RIGHT GROOM

SILHOUETTE *Desire*®

Published by Silhouette Books

America's Publisher of Contemporary Romance

SILHOUETTE BOOKS

ISBN 0-373-76037-X

WRONG BRIDE, RIGHT GROOM

Copyright © 1996 by Merline Lovelace

Printed in U.S.A.

MERLINE LOVELACE

As a career air force officer, Merline Lovelace served tours of duty in Vietnam, at the Pentagon and at bases all over the world. During her years in uniform, she met and married her own handsome hero and stored up enough adventures to keep her fingers flying over the keyboard for years to come. When not glued to the word processor, Merline goes antiquing with her husband, Al, or chases little white balls around the golf courses of Oklahoma.

Merline loves to read and write sizzling contemporaries and sweeping historical sagas. Look for her next book in the Holiday Honeymoons series, coming in February from Silhouette Intimate Moments. She enjoys hearing from readers and can be reached at PO Box 892717, Oklahoma City, OK 73189.

To my mom, Alyce Thoma, who packed up her house and her kids and her dreams every time Dad got transferred. You made a home filled with love and laughter for us wherever we ended up. Thanks, Mom, for all that and so much more.

Prologue

A long, melodramatic sigh carried over the clatter of keyboards and distant mutter of travel agents caught up in the frenzy of last minute Thanksgiving bookings. Lucy Falco, office manager of Gulliver's Travels, tugged her gaze from her flickering computer screen and smiled at the travel agent hovering just outside her office.

"What's up, Tiffany?"

A slender woman with a wild mane of silver curls strolled into the office, her pale gray eyes dancing under a layer of rather startling plum eye shadow. With a girlish grace that belied her sixty-plus years, Tiffany Tarrington Toulouse settled into a tall wingback chair.

"I've worked out the honeymoon package Mr. Gulliver asked us to put together for Abigail Davis's sister." She paused dramatically. "I got them the honeymoon cottage at the Pines."

Lucy's dark brows soared. "The Pines Resort?"

"And at a substantial discount, too."

"How in the world did you manage that?"

"Not very easily! But Abby performed such miracles with our offices, I was determined to come up with something special for her sister."

Tiffany's appreciative gaze roamed Lucy's office, recently redecorated by Abby Davis. The young estate appraiser and antique dealer had transformed Lucy's functional work center into an inviting haven with hunter-green walls, gilt-framed prints, wingback chairs and an antique leather-topped desk in burled cherry. She'd worked the same magic on the rest of Gulliver's Travels, including Tiffany's corner suite, which was why the older agent had worked so hard to put together a special package for her.

"Poor Abby," she said with a shake of her silver curls. "Her sister sprang this wedding on her less than a week ago, then dumped all the arrangements in her lap. I had a time pulling it all together, I can tell you. Every first-class inn and hotel within a hundred miles of Atlanta has been booked up for months, because of the big football game."

Lucy nodded sympathetically. The holidays were always their busiest time. The Georgia-Georgia Tech shoot-out on Thanksgiving Day only added to the chaos. Tiffany had pulled off a real coup by booking the honeymoon couple into the exclusive Pines Inn and Golf Resort, just fifteen miles north of Atlanta.

Still, remembering the near-disastrous Halloween honeymoon package Gulliver's Travels had put together for another couple recently, Lucy wanted reassurance.

"You're sure everything's confirmed?"

"I'm sure."

"You got it in writing?"

"Every detail."

Holding up a ringed hand, the older woman ticked off the arrangements.

"The groom arrives this afternoon. It took some doing, but between us, Beth and I got him an upgrade on a flight out of London. The wedding takes place this evening. The Pines helped us track down a justice of the peace who'll perform the ceremony."

"A real one, I hope," Lucy interjected, the Halloween fiasco still fresh in her mind.

Silvery locks bouncing, Tiffany nodded. "A real one. Afterward, they'll enjoy a private dinner prepared by the inn's world-class chef. Then—" she handed Lucy a colorful brochure "—a honeymoon cottage, complete with wet bar, Jacuzzi, wood-burning fireplace. And one very huge, very decadent bed."

Lucy's dark eyes lit with laughter as she studied the picture. "It's certainly huge, anyway."

"And tomorrow," Tiffany continued gleefully, "the Pines's year-in-advance-reservations-only gourmet Thanksgiving dinner, delivered to the cottage, compliments of Gulliver's Travels.''

Smiling, Lucy handed back the brochure. ''You and Abby certainly went all out. I hope her sister appreciates your efforts.''

''I'm sure she will. This is one honeymoon the bride and groom will never forget!''

One

"What do you mean, you can't marry him?"

Abigail Davis gripped the handle of the 1930s-style white plastic phone and fought to control her exasperation. Losing her temper never did any good. Not with Beth.

"I just can't." Panic laced her younger sister's voice. "I . . . I don't know him."

Turning her back on the two well-dressed matrons browsing through the antique shop, Abby rolled her eyes. *She'd* said exactly the same thing—several times!—when Beth called to announce that she'd met the man of her dreams during an unexpected crew layover in England. By the time her flight crew had been assigned to another international run, the impetuous, impulsive Beth had fallen passionately in love. For the umpteenth time.

Now, after begging Abby's help in arranging a wedding during the brief window of opportunity when she and her air force fiancé would both be in the States, Beth was backing out. Again.

"I'm sorry, Abby. I know how much trouble you went through to set this up for me."

An understatement if ever there was one! Abby bit back a groan, thinking of the frantic phone calls she'd made to Tiffany, not to mention the substantial deposit she'd already paid the Pines to guarantee the honeymoon cottage and the wedding supper. If the wedding was canceled now, she'd be lucky if all she lost was her deposit.

Still, she'd rather forfeit the entire cost of the wedding than see her sister make a serious mistake. Swallowing her irritation, she softened her tone.

"I'm glad you had the courage to face your doubts before the wedding, instead of after."

Relief added a breathless baby-doll quality to Beth's voice. "I knew you'd understand."

"I just hope your groom does."

"He will . . . when you explain it to him."

"What?" Abby shook her head, setting the tendrils of her loosely piled honey-blond hair dancing. "No way, kiddo! I'm not bailing you out of this one."

Her sharp retort drew startled glances from two browsers and a frown from her boss. Marissa DeVries maintained a standing rule against her employees taking personal phone calls while on the floor. That was only one of the many reasons Abby was looking forward to terminating her employment at Things Past.

"Please, Abby."

She hardened her heart against the plea in her sister's voice. "No, Beth."

"Just go to the airport this afternoon and meet Jordy's plane. I ... I can't face him."

At the small, hiccuping sob, a hint of amused exasperation came into Abby's brown eyes. She'd heard that pathetic little sound many times over the years. Usually just before Beth confessed to some childish prank or another, which Abby would end up taking the blame for.

But Beth wasn't a child any longer. And running out on her groom the day of their wedding hardly qualified as a childish prank.

"I won't do it," Abby stated in her best no-nonsense big-sister tone. "If you insist on getting engaged every time you date a man more than once, you can darn well learn to get yourself unengaged."

"You *know* how I hate to hurt anyone's feelings...."

"For heaven's sake, Bethany! We're not talking about just anyone. The man is on a plane at this very moment, flying in from England to marry you."

"I know, I know!" Beth wailed.

"You have to meet him and tell him about your change of heart."

"I can't." There was a small silence, followed by a rushed, guilty admission. "My flight leaves in twenty minutes."

"Flight?" Abby squawked. "What flight?"

"I volunteered to fill in on a Paris-Cairo-Singapore run."

"Beth!" The irritation Abby had squelched just moments ago came rushing back in full force. "Don't you dare skip out on your fiancé. Or on me!"

"Talk to him, Abby. Tell him I'm sorry. Tell him I'll write and explain things."

"No. Absolutely not. I won't—"

"They're calling my flight. I love you, Sissy."

"Don't 'Sissy' me. Not this time. Beth? Bethany?" Abby stretched the receiver out at arm's length, glaring at the marble-grained white plastic.

She couldn't believe it! Beth had done it again. Slipped away and left her to clean up yet another mess. She knew darn well Abby wouldn't let Sergeant Doug Jordan wander Atlanta's busy airport, searching hopelessly for his missing bride.

Dammit!

"If you're quite through with your personal calls, Abigail, you might think about getting back to work."

With some effort, Abby refrained from slamming the receiver into its cradle. She dragged in a steadying breath and turned to face her employer.

As she met Marissa's haughty stare, she told herself she should be grateful to the woman. She'd given Abby a job when she arrived in Atlanta five years ago with her younger sister, a self-taught knowledge of antiques and a burning desire to put down roots.

Abby had always known exactly what kind of roots she wanted. The old-fashioned kind. The kind that went way down deep and included two, or maybe three, generations taught by the same fourth-grade teacher. Sunday-morning pancake breakfasts at the local fire station. A house that wore its age like a welcome mat. Rooms of lovingly polished furniture proudly displaying their scars of use.

The job at Things Past had been Abby's major step toward achieving her dream. At the time, her knowledge of antiques had consisted entirely of a wealth of information gleaned from books and a deep, intrinsic love of all things that possessed the past she and Beth lacked.

Since then, however, she'd learned the business inside and out, been licensed by the state insurance board as an appraiser and increased the shop's inventory through ever more skillful buys. In the process, she'd also worked more hours than any other employee, with marginal recompense and even less recognition. Marissa wasn't the kind of woman to acknowledge anyone's efforts but her own.

"You're taking off early this afternoon to help your sister prepare for her wedding," the raven-haired shop owner said icily. "Do you think you might give Things Past a little attention until then?"

Abby wasn't ready to explain the latest development in the on-again, off-again wedding to her employer, who resented Beth's demands on Abby's time almost as much as the younger woman disliked the supercilious shop owner. Abby suspected one of the reasons her sister had insisted on a small, intimate, family-only wedding was to avoid inviting Marissa.

"Actually," she told her boss, "I need to take off earlier than anticipated. I've got to meet Beth's fiancé at the airport."

"That's out of the question. Your sister knows very well the holiday season is our busiest time of year." Lowering her voice, Marissa nodded toward the two women examining a case of pink Depression glassware. "What's more, the football game is bringing in all kinds of wealthy alumni. I need you here."

"I only came in at all as a special favor to you," Abby reminded her patiently. "I have a lot to do today."

Like cancel a wedding.

Marissa's sharp, elegant features took on a peevish cast. "Beth knew how busy we'd be today. She should have exhibited a bit more consideration in making these hasty wedding plans."

"I doubt if Beth was thinking about the shop when she fell in love and decided to get married," Abby said dryly.

Or when she fell *out* of love, she added with a silent grimace.

While Marissa huffed and complained a bit more, Abby stole a quick glance at her watch. She didn't have the time to humor her humorless employer. Or the patience.

Maybe this little confrontation was for the best, she decided. She was ready to cut the cord. She'd planned to wait until after Beth's wedding to give notice, but she might just as well do it now.

Her sister might have changed her plans for the future. Abby hadn't.

"I'm sorry," she said firmly, interrupting her employer in midcomplaint. "I can't give you any more time today. Or any other day, after the first of December."

Marissa's penciled brows sliced sharply downward. "What do you mean?"

"I told you a few months ago I was thinking about starting my own business."

"Don't be ridiculous. You don't have the capital or the expertise to launch yourself in this business."

"Yes, I do."

The calm rejoinder took the older woman aback. Her heavily mascaraed eyes narrowed as she stared at her employee.

"I've made an offer on a house on Peabody Street," Abby said evenly, hugging to herself the tingle of excitement just saying the words aloud caused. "If the offer's accepted, as the Realtor assures me it will, I plan to open the Painted Door just after the first of the year."

Abby didn't expect congratulations or good wishes, which was just as well, since she received neither. Marissa's lips tightened to a thin scarlet line. Without another word, she turned and walked back to the customers.

Torn between relief at having given notice, simmering exasperation with Beth and near panic at all she had to do in the next few hours, Abby headed for the room at the back of the shop. Another quick glance at her watch told her she'd didn't have time to call Gulliver's Travels and get Tiffany working on the cancellation. Maybe she could reach her from the airport.

She grabbed her purse from the middle drawer of the rolltop desk, then swirled a long black wool cape over her lacy-collared dress. A treasured find at an estate sale some years ago, the cloak served both everyday and evening duty during the chill winter months. Throwing one edge of the cloak over her shoulder, she dashed for the back door.

The moment she stepped outside, icy rain hit her in the face. Gasping, Abby huddled under the overhang, buried her nose in the cape's soft mohair lining and viewed the pelting sleet with dismay. Every few years, a horrendous winter storm swept down from the Great Smoky Mountains to the north and paralyzed the entire Atlanta area. She only hoped this gray, icy drizzle wasn't the precursor of another monster.

The narrow heels of her high-topped granny boots clicked on slick cobblestones as she picked her way to her minivan. Christened the Antiquemobile by Beth some years ago, more for its age than its utilitarian purpose, the brown van huddled in the cold like a fat, forlorn partridge. By the time Abby climbed inside, rain had drizzled down her neck and dampened the lace collar of her dress. Muttering dire imprecations against younger sisters in general and mercurial, impulsive ones in particular, she cranked the key. The engine coughed a few times, then caught. Clutching the wheel with both hands, she backed out of her parking space.

Or tried to.

The van's worn tires whirred alarmingly on slick pavement. Gulping, Abby let up on the foot pedal, then depressed it more slowly. To her relief, the van inched backward. She swung it around, shifted into drive and eased onto the street. Once into the stream of traffic heading south to the interstate, she jiggled the heater's switch. The air blower sputtered once or twice, then wheezed in defeat.

"Wonderful," she muttered as the damp chill whirled through the van. "Just wonderful!"

The tip of her nose tingling with cold, she headed for Atlanta's Hartsfield International Airport. On the way, she sorted through the long list of glowing adjectives Beth had used to describe her fiancé, Technical Sergeant Doug Jordan. It took some effort to turn Beth's ecstatic ramblings into a mental picture of the man she'd meet for the first time in a few minutes.

Tall. Broad-shouldered. Dark-haired and seriously handsome, with an angel's smile and a devilish gleam in his eyes. According to her sister, Jordy filled out his air force uniform like a Greek god and carried himself with an air of utter self-confidence that came with being a member of the air force's elite combat pararescue force—whatever that was. Abby just hoped Sergeant Jordan's self-confidence was up to being left at the proverbial altar.

She arrived at the airport an agonizing forty-five minutes later, wound as tight as a coil by the slippery roads and heavy traffic. Breathless, she dodged hordes of holiday travelers and reached the international gate area just moments after the announcement heralding the arrival of Delta's flight 73 from Heathrow.

No one in uniform, godlike or otherwise, lingered in the waiting room just outside the customs checkpoint. Chewing her lower lip, Abby searched the crowds. From the corner of one eye, she glimpsed the head and shoulders of a tall figure in a brown leather bomber jacket. Abby's first clue that this might be her man was the tight stretch of the leather across his broad shoulders. The second was the razor-short military cut of his dark brown hair. But it was his unmistakable air of authority that clinched the matter in her mind. Although he moved along with the stream of travelers, he seemed to hold himself aloof, apart, much as the leader of a pack would.

"Jordy?"

Abby's call got lost in the waves of noise filling the thronged concourse. Flushed and still breathless from her mad dash through the airport, she hurried after the man. A few steps later, she caught hold of a patch of well-worn leather and tugged.

"Jordy?"

He swung around.

"I'm Abigail, Beth's sis—"

She broke off as eyes so dark a blue they appeared almost black ate into her. Involuntarily she retreated a step.

If this was Doug Jordan, Beth needed to work on her descriptive abilities. None of the adjectives she'd blithely tossed around fit this man. He sported a square, uncompromising jaw, a firm mouth, and a nose that had been broken once too often in the past. The rugged combination was arresting, but certainly didn't come close to handsome in Abby's book.

She had no idea whether his smile could be classified as angelic, since he wasn't wearing one, but the glint in his eyes could easily be considered devilish. He was older than Abby had assumed Doug Jordan would be. Well past thirty, she guessed, although the lines webbing the corners of his eyes could as well have been stamped there by experience as by age.

"You're Abby?" he responded with a lift of one dark brow. "Beth's sister?"

His deep, gravelly voice sent an unexpected shiver down her spine. No wonder Beth didn't have the nerve to face him, she thought. This wasn't the kind of man anyone shrugged off casually.

The midnight-blue eyes raked her from the top of her damp, wildly curling hair to the tips of her granny shoes. When he brought his gaze back to her face, it held a bold, masculine approval that sent an electrical shock skimming along Abby's nerves.

Her shock quickly gave way to a jolt of anger. An engaged man had no business giving anyone except his fiancée that particular look, she thought indignantly. Before she could tell him so, however, he shifted his leather carryall to his left hand. Then, to her utter amazement, he swept her up against his chest and covered her mouth with his own.

His lips were hard, as hard as the rest of the body pressed against hers. And warm. And altogether too seductive for a man about to be married.

Stunned, Abby registered the faint tang of a spicy after-shave. The smoky taste of Scotch. The feel of a big, callused hand cradling the back of her head. When his lips moved over hers, deepening the kiss, astonishment erupted into a hundred different emotions, not the least of which was fury.

Pete heard a muffled squeak, and felt the woman in his arms squirm. Firm breasts, discernible even through layers of wool cloak and leather jacket, pressed against his chest. Sudden, spine-stiffening awareness hammered through him, along with the realization that the brotherly kiss Doug Jordan had asked him to deliver to his new sister-in-law had slipped right past brotherly and was hovering somewhere around explosive.

It had started out innocently enough. Pete hadn't intended anything more than a good-natured exchange. A warm greeting. But her lips were sweeter than anything he'd tasted in a long, long time, and he discovered that he didn't want to release them.

Reluctantly he lifted his head and loosened the arm he'd wrapped around her waist. She jerked backward, leaving the scent of damp wool and flowery perfume behind. The glare she zinged at him packed twice the firepower of a Sidewinder missile.

"Are you crazy, or do prospective in-laws customarily assault each other where you come from?"

"Not customarily, but then, I'm not a prospective in-law."

Her eyes narrowed dangerously. "You're not Doug Jordan?"

"No, ma'am." He sketched a salute with the tips of two fingers. "Senior Master Sergeant Pete O'Brian, at your service. I'm Jordy's supervisor."

"His supervisor?"

"I'm afraid Jordy couldn't make it back to the States."

"Couldn't make it!" she echoed blankly. "Why not? Where is he?"

He thought for a moment. "About two thousand feet over a very cold, very hostile little country, about to jump into the middle of a civil war. Our unit got orders to deploy just an hour before Jordy was supposed to leave for home."

"Good grief! Didn't the fact that he was supposed to get married today make any difference?"

Pete lifted a brow at her faintly accusing look. "Not to me. Or to him, when the orders came down. Jordy's a professional."

While she digested that one, he glanced around the emptying terminal. "So where's the bride? I have a message for her."

A taut silence brought his gaze swinging back to the woman before him. She pursed her lips, then answered with obvious reluctance.

"About twenty thousand feet over the Atlantic. On her way to Singapore, by way of Paris and Cairo."

"No kidding?" Pete's mouth curled. "Well, what do you know? I bet Jordy she wouldn't show."

"What?"

The bet had just been a joke, although Pete hadn't really expected the ditzy flight attendant Doug Jordan had met during a weekend in London to go through with their hasty marriage plans. From the little he'd seen of Beth Davis, Pete could tell she lacked the depth to live up to her rash promises.

Jordy had fallen for her, though. Fallen hard, despite Pete's caustic suggestion that the young sergeant was just experiencing a healthy dose of male lechery. Which pretty well described the feeling Beth Davis's older sister was stirring in Pete this very minute.

She stood ramrod-stiff before him, arms crossed, brown eyes flashing. She didn't come close to the gut-twisting, throat-closing physical perfection of her sister, of course, but few women did. Pete had been around long enough, however, to recognize that Abigail Davis occupied a class all by herself.

Her wildly curling hair was streaked with every color of the sun, from pale wheat to burnt umber, and her skin glistened with a dewy softness that reminded him of fresh-cut flowers and vanilla pudding. She stood a good six inches less than his own six-one, but that firm, tip-tilted chin warned Pete she didn't consider either his size or his presence particularly significant. Her creamy skin and soft, full mouth pulled at him, though, almost as much as the intelligence in her brown eyes. Obviously, Abby Davis possessed more than her younger sister's thimbleful of common sense.

And, just as obviously, she wasn't letting him off the hook. A delicately arched brow a few shades darker than her tawny hair lifted.

"You were about to explain this bet?"

"Considering the fact that the bride and groom had known each other less than thirty-six hours, it was a pretty safe bet. I know Jordy. When he makes up his mind, there's no changing it. But your sister didn't strike me as . . ."

"As what?"

The slight narrowing of her doe eyes should have alerted Pete. If he'd had any sleep at all in the past seventy-two hours, he probably wouldn't have missed the danger signal. But the bunged-up knee that had kept him from participating in the short-notice deployment hadn't prevented him from overseeing the preparations for it. After a marathon round-the-clock planning session, he'd put Jordy and the rest of his squad on a transport plane, just hours before he had to leave for the States himself. Then he'd spent most of the long flight home reworking the ops plan in his mind, trying to convince himself that he hadn't sent his men into a political and military quagmire with no escape route. Weariness now dragged at him like beggars in a back alley, and made him finish with more truth than diplomacy.

"She didn't strike me as the steady, reliable type," he said with a small shrug.

Abby bristled. Beth had her faults, which she'd have been the first to admit. Whatever she lacked in common sense or staying power, however, she more than made up for in spontaneity and warmth. Those she loved, she loved generously and unconditionally. Unfortunately, she tended to fall out of love as frequently as she fell into it.

As Abby knew better than anyone, that instability stemmed from their childhood. Beth had been so much younger when their parents died in a car accident. She'd learned to transfer her affections as easily as a puppy, first to the aunt who took the Davis girls in, then to the series of foster homes they were sent to when their widowed aunt proved emotionally incapable of raising two children. Over the years, the bond between the sisters had proven the only bedrock in their transient lives.

That bond had seen them through the difficult years, until Abby turned eighteen, got a full-time job, rented her first apartment and petitioned the court for custody of her younger sister. Ten years later, it still shaped Abby's life, and served as Beth's safety net in situations like this.

"I wouldn't be so quick to disparage my sister," she replied acidly. "After all, Doug Jordan didn't show up for his own wedding, either."

O'Brian's smirk faded. "The circumstances are entirely different. In Jordy's case, it was a matter of duty."

"I'm not sure I think very much of a man who puts duty before his wife."

"I wouldn't think very much of a man who didn't."

Their eyes locked, dark blue flint striking sparks off angry brown shale.

"What about you?" Abby retorted tartly. "Shouldn't you be off doing your duty?"

He didn't answer right away. When he did, a muscle twitched in his right cheek. "Yes, I should."

She watched the small movement with some surprise. Apparently she'd struck a nerve. He drew in a slow breath, and then a weariness seemed to settle over his face, etching deep lines in the tanned skin.

"Look, I had to come back to the States anyway. Jordy asked me to swing through Atlanta and explain his deployment to Beth. He also wanted me to tell her..." His jaw worked. "To tell her that he loves her."

The words came out with a rusty edge, as though it pained him to acknowledge anything as human as emotion.

Abby winced inwardly. In her irritation with O'Brian, she'd forgotten the other emotions involved in this little drama. Darn her sister, anyway.

"I'll give Beth the message."

O'Brian nodded, hefting his carryall. "Guess I'd better go find a cab and a hotel. It's been a long flight."

Thinking of the thousands of football fans and holiday travelers thronging the city, Abby hesitated.

"You don't have a hotel reservation?"

"No, I changed my flight at the last minute to get to Atlanta. I'll find something, though." He tipped her another salute. "Nice meeting you, Abigail."

She couldn't quite bring herself to return the polite sentiment. "Happy Thanksgiving . . . er . . ."

"Pete."

"Pete."

He was a good ten yards away before she noticed his uneven gait. Frowning, she shifted a few paces to one side and followed his progress down the concourse. It was more than just an uneven gait, she discovered. O'Brian walked with a decided limp. He held himself so erect and square-shouldered, it wasn't noticeable immediately, but now that she focused on it, she wondered how she could have missed it earlier.

As she watched him move away, embarrassment flooded through her. Oh, nice going, Abby! Nothing like deriding the man for not doing his so-called duty when he'd obviously been injured in some way, then sending him on his way, a stranger in an unfamiliar city.

Resolutely Abby quashed her guilt. Hey, he wasn't her responsibility. Having felt a few of his sharp edges, she'd be surprised if he was anyone's responsibility but his own.

Still, he had gone out of his way to do a favor for Jordy and Beth. He was going to have a heck of time finding anyplace to stay tonight . . . and she did happen to have a honeymoon cottage reserved.

She glanced at her watch and barely stifled a groan. There was no way she'd get back her hefty deposit on the cottage, not at this late hour. Nor would she recoup any of the sunk costs for the two-tiered chocolate-rum-raisin wedding cake Beth had requested. Or for the crown rib roast and delicate onion soufflé the Pines's chef was probably preparing at this very moment.

Her gaze swung to a disappearing patch of brown leather.

Darn Beth anyway!

Two

Abby caught up with O'Brian while he waited for the shuttle to the main terminal. He acknowledged her appearance at his side with a quirk of one dark brow.

"I don't know how long you plan to be in the Atlanta area...." she began hesitantly.

"A few days. When I changed my reservations, I had to take a layover I hadn't planned on."

"You might have trouble finding a place to stay. The big Georgia-Georgia Tech game is tomorrow. The city's under siege by sixty thousand or so avid fans."

A glimmer of something that might have been amusement stirred in his deep cobalt eyes. "I've slept on everything from a moving ice floe to a tree limb sixty feet above the jungle floor. If I have to, I can make myself comfortable on a park bench.''

She would have written Mr. Macho off then and there, if his amusement hadn't evolved into a slow, crooked and totally unexpected grin.

''Thanks for the warning, though.''

Abby blinked. Good grief! When he smiled, really smiled, those rugged features came dangerously close to handsome, after all.

She was still dealing with the impact of that devastating arrangement of his facial features when the shuttle whooshed to a halt at the edge of the platform. An impatient traveler jockeyed for position, inadvertently thumping her suitcase into his right leg. Before Abby's eyes, O'Brian's heart-thumping grin twisted into an involuntary grimace. His knee buckled, and he wobbled for an instant.

She caught his arm with both hands, concern lancing through her. Beth would have recognized the ''mother'' look on her face instantly.

''Are you all right?''

He righted himself. ''Yes.''

Her fingers curled into the soft leather sleeve. He didn't look all right. Not with those deep grooves slashing into the skin at the sides of his mouth and his eyes gone hard and flat.

''Are you sure?''

The tight, closed look on his face gave way to a flicker of annoyance. He reversed their roles, tugging his arm free to take hers instead.

"I'm fine. Just feeling a little jet lag." He guided her across the platform. "Watch your step here."

She wedged herself into the shuttle car and snagged a few inches of hand space on a shiny metal pole. He followed, bracing a hand high above hers. His body bracketed hers. To Abby's consternation, his scent seemed to envelop her. She suspected she'd never again catch a whiff of fine-grained leather without thinking of this man. And his kiss.

As furious as that kiss had made her at the time, in retrospect she had to admit it ranked right up there among the top dozen or so she'd received. Well, maybe among the top three.

Come on! Who was she kidding? She'd never been kissed like that, not even by the man she'd thought she loved.

No nun, Abby had managed to squeeze in a semirespectable social life while struggling to get Beth through college and flight school, putting in long hours at work and studying for her licensing as an appraiser. Along the way, she'd experienced her share of male embraces. Some had left her breathless. A few had made her ache for more. One man's had made her think she'd found the permanency that had eluded her since her parents' death.

It wasn't anyone's fault that Derek's interest had swung from the older sister to the younger the day Beth breezed back into Atlanta after a four-month rotation in South America. She was so beautiful, so full of mischief and life, few men could resist her. Derek couldn't, anyway.

His handsome image drifted through Abby's mind, surprisingly hazy and indistinct. She was congratulating herself on the fact that thinking about him occasioned nothing more than a mild twinge of regret when the shuttle car jerked forward.

Her shoulder bumped Pete's chest.

His hips nudged hers.

Intimately.

For several long seconds, she felt the length of him against her back and bottom. A suffocating heat that had nothing to do with the warmth in the jammed car climbed up Abby's neck. Flustered, she pressed closer to the metal upright. The swaying, jostling crowd defeated her best efforts to preserve a modicum of airspace between her and the man behind her, however. By the time the underground train glided to a halt at the main terminal, she felt as stiff and compressed as corrugated cardboard.

A firm hold on her elbow steadied her against the buffeting streams of pedestrians pouring out of the shuttle. Abby felt his strength right through her layers of wool and mohair. Frowning slightly over her reaction to this stranger, she paced beside him. They were halfway through the main terminal before she recalled her reason for catching up with him in the first place.

"I booked a room—well, a cottage, actually—for Jordy and Beth at the Pines Inn and Resort. You're welcome to use it."

He glanced down at her, polite refusal forming in his eyes. Shrewdly Abby guessed he didn't like accepting favors. From anyone. Then his dark blue gaze swept the jam-packed terminal.

"Maybe I'll take you up on the offer," he said slowly. "That's the Pines, right?"

"Right. I should warn you, though, it's about fifteen miles north of the city."

"No problem, as long a taxi driver can find it." He slowed to a halt a few yards from the main exit and extended his hand. "Thanks, Abigail."

She put her palm in his, absorbing the heat and roughness of his skin against hers.

"You're welcome."

He hesitated, and then his mouth hitched in that crooked smile. "About that kiss a while ago. It was out of line. Way out of line."

"You're right. It was."

"I should apologize."

She arched a brow. "Yes, you should."

"The problem is, I'm not sorry."

Now that her anger had cooled, Abby wasn't all that sorry, either. But that wasn't something a woman admitted to a man she'd only met a few minutes ago. One she wasn't even sure she liked.

"Would you accept dinner instead of an apology?"

As soon as the words were out of his mouth, Pete could have kicked himself. He needed sleep, about two or three days' worth. Even more important, he needed to nip this reluctant attraction he felt for Abigail Davis in the bud. One look at her had been enough to tell Pete she wasn't his type.

Although the lady certainly didn't pull any punches, she had that warm, delicious, *womanly* aura that spelled big trouble to any man with enough sense to recognize it. Unlike her fun-loving sister, Abby Davis no doubt expected more from a man than a weekend in Soho. Everything about her shouted quality. And respect. And permanence. The kind of permanence that came with long-term relationships, maybe even marriage.

Pete had learned the hard way that there wasn't anything permanent in a military marriage. Not in his, anyway. It had been plagued from the start by too many absences, too few joyful reunions. After the stormy breakup eight years ago, he'd sworn to avoid the kind of relationships that demanded more time and attention than he could give them while he wore a uniform. Which meant, he decided with a flicker of real regret, avoiding women like Abby Davis.

From the uncertainty chasing across her face, she didn't appear too thrilled with the prospect of having dinner with him, either. He couldn't blame her. Not after the way he'd manhandled her. Before he could think of a graceful way to withdraw his offer, however, she took him up on it. More or less.

"I'll tell you what. There's a nine-course wedding dinner and a chocolate-rum-raisin wedding cake waiting for the missing bride and groom at the Pines. Why don't we share the dinner, so we can tell our respective sister and subordinate what they missed later?"

"You've got a deal."

* * *

Abby regretted the offer the moment she stepped outside the terminal. Icy sleet drummed down on the overhead canopy with a tinny staccato beat. Alarming little mounds of slush were piled up along the pavement. It splashed over her feet whenever a car whooshed by. What was more, the lowering gray sky gave every indication that the storm was only going to get worse.

Shoulders hunched against the piercing wind, she jammed her hands in her pockets and waited for the bus to the parking lot. As she shifted from foot to foot to keep the cold from seeping through her thin soles, she weighed the pros of dinner with Pete O'Brian against the cons of a thirty-mile round-trip in this mess.

She was careful by nature, and overly cautious as a result of years of acting as a foil for the high-strung, effervescent Beth. Her every instinct screamed at her to back out of the trip to the Pines. The sensible thing to do would be to inch her way home through the heavy traffic and curl up with a good book under the down-filled comforter that covered her iron bedstead.

She was framing the words to renege on her offer when the parking-lot shuttle bus pulled up. Once inside, Pete settled his long frame on the seat beside her, stashed his carryall under his legs and reached down with a strong, blunt-fingered hand to massage his knee.

Abby frowned, then looked up and caught his glance. This time, she wasn't about to let him off with the excuse of jet lag.

"I made a bad jump a few weeks ago," he muttered, reading her expression. "Hit the ground a little harder than I'd intended to."

"A jump? You mean, like out of a plane?"

Nodding, he tucked his hand into his jacket pocket and eased his shoulders back against the seat. Abby found herself squeezed between his solid frame and a portly Georgia football fan in a red ball cap with an equally portly bulldog emblazoned on its bill.

"Do you do that often?" she asked, edging sideways to keep her hips and thighs from bumping O'Brian's. "Jump out of planes, I mean?"

"I guess that depends on your definition of *often*. Sometimes we go for months with nothing but our requal jumps. Other times, it seems like we're popping the chutes every week."

"Once would be too often for me," Abby admitted, shuddering. "For the life of me, I can't understand why anyone would want to jump out of an airplane that wasn't diving straight down."

He slanted her an amused glance. "If it was diving straight down, your chances of jumping out would be pretty slim."

The sound of an audible gulp brought their heads around.

"I'm flying back to Schenectady after the game tomorrow," the portly football fan next to her said sheepishly. "Would you two mind talking about something other than planes going down?"

Pete laughed and obligingly changed the subject to the odds of the Bulldogs' awesome offense plowing right through Georgia Tech's injury-ridden defensive line. The others on the bus were quick to add their opinions, and the conversation soon degenerated into an unabashedly partisan debate. Although Abby had her own opinions about Georgia's so-called power-house offense, she let the lively discussion flow around her. She much preferred to watch Pete's face as he refereed the debate.

It was an intriguing one, she decided again, with character stamped in the lines fanning from the corners of his eyes and bracketing his mouth. Character and, she guessed, perhaps a residue of pain. Obviously he still hadn't recovered from that bad jump he mentioned, which no doubt explained why he hadn't accompanied Jordy and the rest of his unit on their unexpected deployment. Maybe he'd come back to the States on convalescent leave. Idly Abby wondered how long he'd be in the States...and who he might have left behind in England.

The thought jerked her out of her contemplation of his strong, firm chin and bumpy nose. Startled, she realized she'd agreed to have dinner with a man she knew absolutely nothing about. He might very well have a wife and three kids waiting for him overseas.

She frowned, trying to remember whether the hands tucked in his jacket pockets sported any rings of the plain-gold-band variety. She didn't think so, but that didn't mean much these days. For safety reasons, a good number of men and women in hazardous professions didn't wear rings. Jumping out of airplanes ranked right up there among the most hazardous, in Abby's book.

Nor did that bone-melting kiss rule out the possibility that he was otherwise attached. Abby hadn't tangled with many married men on the prowl, but she'd come across one or two in her time. Her frown deepening, she stole another glance at Pete O'Brian's face. She didn't know why, but she couldn't bring herself to believe he was a member of that particular subspecies. She'd make it a point to find out, though, over dinner.

It wasn't until she was unlocking the door to the Antiquemobile that Abby realized she'd unconsciously decided to make the drive to the Pines after all. Well, she could only hope the weather didn't worsen and make her regret her decision.

Gripping the wheel with tight fists, she eased out of the parking lot and into the stream of traffic heading north on slick, slush-covered roads. She breathed a quiet sigh of relief when the slush splattered and disappeared under the churning tires. The stuff was ugly, but not icy.

"I'm sorry the heater doesn't work," she murmured, hunching her shoulders against the frigid air in the van. "It went out a few years ago, and I never bothered to get it fixed. We don't usually get this kind of weather in Atlanta."

She threw him a quick smile. "Although I suppose it doesn't faze a man who slept on an ice floe."

Pete smiled back, but his eyes held concern as he surveyed the gray drizzle on the windshield.

"Maybe driving to the Pines isn't such a good idea. I don't like taking you so far out of your way, especially on roads like this."

"They're not as bad as I was afraid they'd be. I don't think we'll have any problem."

Careful, cautious Abby mentally crossed all ten fingers, and those of her toes that weren't frozen from the cold and dampness. She would have worried herself to a quiet frazzle if Beth had been the one out driving in this kind of weather.

"Besides, I really need to speak to the manager. The chocolate-rum-raisin cake's already paid for, but maybe there's a chance I can recoup a few of the other costs of this unwedding."

"Are you saying your sister left you holding the bag *and* the bill when she backed out on Jordy?"

Abby dragged her gaze from the road and leveled him a look as frosty as the air in the van. "I think we'd better settle something right now, O'Brian. My sister isn't perfect, I admit, but I won't tolerate criticism of her, particularly from someone who doesn't even know her."

He didn't take offense at her blunt speaking. If anything, Abby thought she caught a glint of approval in his dark eyes. Military men, she supposed, appreciated the concepts of loyalty and brotherhood. Or, in this case, sisterhood.

"Fair enough," he replied. "For the record, though, I do know Beth. Or maybe I should say I've met her. I was with Jordy the weekend he bumped into her and—" his mouth curled downward "—went off the deep end."

"That's one way to put it," she agreed, relenting a little. Personally, she'd used a few stronger phrases during the nights she tossed and turned and fretted over Beth's rash decision to marry a near stranger.

"It's the only polite way to put it."

Abby shot him a quick glance. "I take it you don't subscribe to the theory of love at first sight?"

"No. Lust at first sight, maybe. The right mix of chemicals will always generate a spontaneous combustion, but that kind of fire flares hot, and usually burns out fast."

Abby suspected he spoke from personal experience. Given the way he'd ignited tiny flames in her blood within seconds of their meeting, he'd probably sparked his fair share of good-size conflagrations with other, more willing partners. Still, the cynicism in his reply bothered her.

"Is that what you think love is?" she asked curiously. "A purely chemical reaction?"

"What else?"

"I don't know," she murmured, more to herself than to him. "But I hope it's more. Much more."

Deciding that the conversation had drifted into far-too-personal channels, she steered it toward the soaring Atlanta skyline on their left. Tomorrow's big game. The unusual weather.

Pete followed her lead, his hands shoved into his pockets and his long legs stretched out as far as the van would allow. The fact that the lady didn't have any better definition than he did of the hazy, indefinable and, in his opinion, highly overrated emotion called love intrigued him. So she wasn't involved with someone she considered herself in love with.

The thought gave him a twist of pleasure at some deep, visceral level. He wrote off the sensation as a mindless male response to the knowledge that an attractive female was available. An attractive female who just happened to fit in his arms perfectly. One whose sexy, tantalizing mouth would no doubt drift through his dreams tonight.

Regret once again stirred beneath his layers of bone-deep tiredness. Regret, and the realization that one taste of Abby Davis wasn't quite enough to satisfy him. It was just as well that he wouldn't see Doug Jordan's almost-in-law again after tonight. Tasting her could fast become addictive.

Banishing an insidious image of a private feast that included Abby as the main course, Pete responded easily to her conversational gambits. After a few miles, however, he let the conversation die away altogether. The wet roads required her attention. Not wanting to distract her, he crossed his ankles and gave every appearance of being absorbed in the gray landscape outside.

He had plenty of time to absorb it. Rush-hour traffic, and the driving rain slowed the already sluggish pace around Atlanta's busy loop. When they finally exited onto a less busy state road, the traffic moved a little more quickly, but the air in the van grew progressively colder with every mile north they progressed. Gradually the weak afternoon light faded to a purplish gloom. Headlights flickered on. The windshield wipers worked steadily.

By the time they passed through a small village appropriately called Pineville and turned off at tall brick pillars announcing the Pines Inn and Golf Resort, Pete felt distinctly uncomfortable about taking Abby so far out of her way. He didn't say anything while she negotiated the narrow, winding access road that cut through timber-covered hills. But when she pulled up at the sprawling two-story artistry of weathered cedar, native stone and soaring glass that constituted the resort's main lodge, he stopped her before she got out of the van.

"Why don't we pass on dinner?" he suggested. "I don't like the idea of you tackling these roads after dark."

Abby didn't particularly like the idea herself, but she'd come this far. A hot meal—particularly one she'd already paid for—would go a long way toward dispelling the ice crystals in her blood and make the drive home a less daunting prospect.

"I'm here now," she replied with a small shrug. "I might as well indulge myself with a taste of that rum-raisin cake before heading home."

"You can take it with you. Or," he amended slowly, his eyes holding hers, "you could stay at the inn tonight. That way, I wouldn't have to worry about you driving home alone—and we could share an unwedding breakfast, in addition to dinner."

Abby stared at him, her jaw sagging. Then she gave herself a mental shake. For heaven's sake, the man wasn't suggesting she spend the night with him.

Was he?

She peered at him through the gloom. For the life of her, she couldn't tell. His face was in shadows, and his eyes were a deep, impenetrable black. She opted for a neutral response.

"I doubt if they'll have room. We only got the honeymoon cottage on such short notice because it's so isolated from the main lodge."

And so outrageously expensive, she added silently. "Let's get you checked in and track down our dinner. Then I'll head home, and you can sleep off your jet lag in a bed you'll have to see to believe."

They walked through the tall, weathered oak doors of the inn and stepped into a scene of total chaos. A chartered busload of University of Georgia alumni, sporting heavily jowled bulldogs on everything from designer jackets to diamond-encrusted pendants, filled every square inch of the lobby. They laughed and chattered among themselves while harried desk clerks tried to sort out what appeared to be a major foul-up in reservations. Leaving Pete to work his way through the amorphous, free-flowing lines, Abby sought out the manager.

He'd left half an hour ago, she soon discovered. As had the special events coordinator. Unable to confirm exactly what charges had been incurred at this point, a distracted assistant manager promised Abby someone would call her tomorrow with concrete figures. He also assured her that he'd notify the justice of the peace who was supposed to perform the ceremony in less than an hour that the wedding was off.

Disappointed that her long trip hadn't produced more concrete results, Abby returned to the lobby. She found Pete a few paces closer to the front desk, still caught in the throng of alumni. At his insistence, she gave him the confirmation number, then slipped off her cloak and settled down to wait in a wingback chair done in rich burgundy fabric.

Palming her hands down the slim, calf-length skirt of her black velveteen dress, she smoothed away the worst of the wrinkles. With its wide collar of delicate Brussels lace and its bone buttons, it would do well enough for dinner at a four-star restaurant. She just wished she could slip off her thin-soled granny boots and massage some warmth back into her frozen feet.

Pete made his way over to her some twenty minutes later, a rueful smile in his eyes and tired lines etched deep in his face.

"I'm checked in, but it's going to be a while yet before I can get to the cabin to clean up. Their shuttle service is overwhelmed at this point." He rasped a hand across a chin stubbled with dark shadows. "If you don't mind waiting another few minutes, I'll find a men's room and scrape off a few layers."

Abby pushed herself out of the chair, ignoring the instant protest from her still-numb toes. "Don't be silly. I'll drive you to the cottage. Besides, I'd like to see if it lives up to its extravagant advertising."

"At these prices, it better," Pete said wryly, shepherding her through the lobby with a hand at the small of her back. The casual touch was probably nothing more than an unconscious gesture on his part, but it sent a sudden dart of awareness through Abby.

"Which reminds me," he added casually. "You'll need to sign the credit slip when we come back."

"Credit slip?"

"For the deposit you put down to guarantee the room. I had them credit your charge card and bill the room to mine."

"You didn't have to do that," she protested. "I offered you the use of the cottage tonight because it was already paid for. I didn't intend for you to get stuck with expensive accommodations you hadn't planned on."

He shrugged off her objections. "As you pointed out, I was lucky to get a room at all. There's no reason for you to foot the bill for me. Or for Jordy, for that matter," he tacked on, propelling her toward the door once more. "I'll talk to him when I get back about the fix this aborted wedding put you in."

"Wait a minute." Abby dug in her heels, a little indignant at his blithe assumption of authority in something that wasn't really any of his business. "You don't need to talk to anyone. The bride's family is responsible for the wedding arrangements, you know."

"I'm sure Jordy didn't realize his ditzy fiancée stuck you with—" He broke off and tried, unsuccessfully, to recover. "Sorry. What I meant is that I know Jordy. He's a solid troop, one of the best in my squad. He'll want to reimburse you for expenses incurred on his behalf."

Abby lifted her chin. Any desire she might have felt to share dinner with this hard-eyed cynical stranger faded in the face of a fierce protectiveness that was as natural to her as breathing.

"Back off, O'Brian. Any expenses I incurred on my *sister's* behalf are no concern of yours. Or anyone else's."

His jaw squared. So did his shoulders.

Abby refused to be intimidated, although she eyed the muscle twitching in his left cheek with a touch of wary interest. The expression in his eyes confirmed the impression she'd formed at the airport that this wasn't a man to cross.

"Have it your way," he conceded, with a distinct lack of graciousness.

"I will."

She spun around and sailed through the crowded lobby. Pete followed, his carryall clenched in one fist. They both halted outside the inn, pinned under the awning by the cold, pelting rain.

"It's not letting up."

The deep voice at her shoulder was still a little clipped around the edges.

"No, it's not." She fished in her purse for her keys. "I think I'd better leave you to handle the rum-raisin cake by yourself, after all."

Abby knew darn well her decision to back out of dinner had more to do with Pete's careless comment about Beth than with the weather. She suspected he knew it, too.

Tough!

She dashed to the van, wondering just what it was about Pete O'Brian that got to her so easily. In the short time she'd known him, she'd run the gamut from astonishment to fury to reluctant awareness to simmering anger once more. Since she'd always considered herself the sober, steady sibling, she didn't understand or particularly like his unsettling affect on her.

It was just as well that she was heading home after she dropped him off at the cottage, Abby decided. The man bothered her, plain and simple. In ways she wasn't up to dealing with tonight.

Following the directions Pete culled from a map of the resort, she circled a huddle of buildings he identified as the golf pro shop and starter shack, then aimed the van up a steep, narrow path. The winding road corkscrewed past the Pines' famous cottages. Shingle-roofed structures the size of a house, they were tucked away amid stands of tall, dark firs. Gritting her teeth, Abby negotiating each switchback turn in the road at a pace a snail could have challenged. When she pulled up at the two-story cottage that sat in solitary splendor atop the crest, she shifted into park, but kept the motor running.

Pete reached for the carryall stashed under his feet, then slewed around in his seat to face her.

"I really think you should reconsider driving home tonight. Stay here. It looks like a big place," he added. "Two stories. We'd have one apiece."

Well, that settled the question of whether his earlier invitation to share the cottage cloaked some ulterior motive. She offered him her hand and a small smile.

"No, thanks. It's all yours."

"You sure?"

"I'm sure."

He searched her face for a moment, then opened the door and eased outside. "I appreciate the lift, Abby."

"It was the least I could do for Jordy's personal messenger."

She waited until Pete had unlocked the cottage door before she put the van in gear. He stood silhouetted in a spill of light from the interior as she drove off, telling herself it was ridiculous to feel this perverse niggle of disappointment at the way the evening had turned out.

Her disappointment quickly gave way to consternation. Some law of physics that she apparently didn't understand made going down steep hills more treacherous than going up. She negotiated the first hairpin turn at a slow crawl, her muscles knotted with tension.

The common sense Abby prided herself on asserted itself before she reached the second turn. If she could have turned the van around on the narrow path, she might have swallowed both her pride and her irritation and taken O'Brian up on his offer. Since she couldn't, she decided she'd stop at the main lodge and wait till this drizzle let up before tackling the drive home.

She never made it to the second turn.

While she was still some yards away, the Antiquemobile hit a slick patch, slid off the road and slammed sideways into a tree.

Three

─────

Pete should have been out by now.

He should have crashed twenty seconds after stepping out of the shower.

When the taillights on Abby's van had disappeared, he'd come inside the cottage and barely glanced at the soaring open-beamed oak ceilings and luxurious furnishings before heading for the loft bedroom. Dumping his gear bag, he'd hit the shower with a sigh of sheer pleasure. He'd returned to the bedroom scant moments later, fully intending to sink into oblivion in the half-acre bed that dominated the spacious loft.

Instead, he found himself standing beside the huge bed, ignoring the weariness that ate into his bones like a sad, sorry song. One corner of his tired mind admired the massive bed frame done in polished oak, metal scrollwork and gleaming brass. A less aesthetic part acknowledged that a bed like this was built to be shared.

With someone like Abby.

His body tightening, Pete gave in to the half-formed fantasy that hovered at the back of his consciousness. It began with the kiss at the airport and took wing. With unswerving male directness, it led to a vision of Abby sprawled across this ocean of royal blue spread, her arms outflung and her honey-streaked hair tumbling in wild abandon. Her brown eyes heavy-lidded. Her soft, full mouth curving in invitation.

Sure, O'Brian. Sure.

That soft, full mouth had chewed him up and spit him out in small, well-masticated pieces during their confrontation in the lobby. For all her refined appearance and warm smile, Abigail Davis could fire up hotter and faster than a phosphorous grenade in defense of that bubbleheaded sister of hers.

Shaking his head, Pete snagged his jeans from the foot of the bed. His bare feet sank into thick wheat-colored carpet as he headed back down the stairs. He was too tired to sleep, he acknowledged. And too irritated by the way his misguided, heavy-handed attempt to make sure Abby didn't get stuck with all the costs of this wedding had backfired on him. He wasn't exactly sure why he even cared, except that the long, cold ride in her decrepit van had convinced him she wasn't exactly rolling in cash.

That, and the fact that his stomach still tightened every time he let himself think about that damned kiss. The memory of her mouth under his pulled at him, as did the woman herself. Despite her prickliness every time her sister's name entered the conversation, or maybe because of it, she characterized everything he admired in a woman and wouldn't let himself respond to.

He liked the way she'd stood up to him. Respected her loyalty to her sister. The sensual appeal in her slender body and delicate, aristocratic features didn't exactly repulse him, either, he admitted with a wry twist of his lips. No wonder he'd felt that kick to the gut when he kissed her, a solid hit he termed lust, for lack of any better description.

Still, he couldn't believe he'd invited her to share this cottage tonight. Twice! Good thing she hadn't taken him up on either invitation. As bone-weary as he was, he wouldn't have gotten much sleep, thinking about Abby all alone in that big bed, and there wasn't much likelihood she'd have shared it with him.

He snapped on a low table lamp and crossed to the oak wall unit at one end of the vast sitting room, confident one of its paneled doors would yield a wet bar stocked with a classy brand of Scotch. He found it on the second try. Splashing a good three fingers into a heavy crystal glass, he took an appreciative sip.

Very classy, he decided as it burned a slow, satisfying line down his throat.

Like Abigail Davis.

He took the Scotch with him to the cavernous stone fireplace, which was conveniently equipped with a gas starter. Within moments, tiny pinpoints of blue flame licked along the stacked logs. Propping a foot on the low stone fender, Pete marveled at the tangled web of circumstance that had led him to an argument over personal finances with a woman he hardly knew.

If Beth hadn't gotten cold feet and skipped out on her wedding.

If Jordy hadn't deployed just hours before he was due to leave for the States.

If Pete hadn't made a downwind landing two weeks ago and torn his anterior cruciate ligament all to hell...

Unconsciously he massaged his knee with a steady, rhythmic motion. He stared into the fire, seeing vivid, pulse-tripping images of that last jump form and re-form in the dancing flames.

The black hole of the open cargo door yawned before him. In his mind's eye, he saw his men go out, one after another. He heard the snick of the static-line clips. The sudden catch in the rhythm. The jumpmaster's frantic shout.

Again and again, he relived the nightmare of trying to retrieve Carrington's body.

With a vicious curse, Pete downed the rest of his Scotch and shoved the glass onto the mantel. The doubts and questions that had plagued him since the accident pounded through his brain. He should have seen that Carrington was too nervous. Should have caught the way his fist had wrapped around the static line. Dammit, he should have...

A sudden banging dragged him from his private hell. He swung around, his muscles coiled, as if in anticipation of attack.

Another thump rattled the front door, and then a wavery voice carried through the solid wood.

"Pete? It's me, Abby. I've... I've had an accident."

He crossed the room in four long strides and wrenched the door open. It went crashing back against the wall. The shivering, bedraggled woman on the doorstep flinched at the violence, then lifted a shaky hand to gesture vaguely behind her.

"The van... in a ditch. I walked..."

Pete's training kicked in before the words were half out of his mouth. Raking her from head to toe with a swift, blade-sharp glance, he cut off her stumbling recital.

"Are you hurt?"

"I... I..."

Her teeth were chattering so hard she couldn't speak. Resisting the impulse to sweep her wet, trembling body into his arms and carry her inside, Pete took a firm grip on her arm instead. She'd walked this far. He wouldn't add to any trauma she might have sustained by jostling her unnecessarily now.

He got her inside, kicked the door shut and peeled her sodden cape from her shoulders. A swift visual showed no protruding bones or obvious hematomas.

"Tell me if you're hurting, Abby."

His voice soothed, calmed, demanded.

"No... I don't..."

He slid his hands under her wet hair and wrapped them around her neck. His skilled fingers found no step-offs, no deformities or abnormalities that might suggest the spinal injuries so common in vehicle accidents. Capturing her cheeks and chin in a firm, gentle vise, he tilted her face toward the light. Her eyes were wide and teary, but the pupils hadn't dilated with shock. Although clammy, the skin under his hands retained enough heat for him to rule out hypothermia.

"I'm not... hurt. Just wet and... cold."

"We'll fix that in a minute."

Holding back the relief that clamored in his veins, Pete swiftly attacked the buttons on the front of her black dress. She closed her hands over his, a startled question in her eyes.

"It's okay. I need to check your ribs."

Swallowing, she dropped her hands.

Pete worked swiftly. In his twenty-two years in rescue, he'd seen too many cases where crew members' minds had selectively shut down to pain while their bodies endured unbelievable trauma. Men had dodged the enemy for hours while carrying their own amputated limbs. Others had crawled incredible distances with the bones in both legs shattered. Abby might well have suffered internal injuries she didn't feel, couldn't acknowledge.

Easing her dress down to her hips, he ran exploring hands over ribs encased in wet black silk. Her heart thumped solidly against his palms. Every rib felt whole and in place. He released the relief he'd been holding back. It flowed through him, a hot, surging wave that made his fingers want to grip the wet silk.

"I don't think you broke anything."

"Yes, I did...." She got the words out through racking shivers. "My van...is all...dented."

Grinning, Pete scooped her up and headed for the stairs, leaving dress and cloak in wet heaps on the floor. "If that's the worst of the damages, I'd say you're in pretty good shape, Ms. Davis."

Very good shape, he amended as she curled into him, seeking warmth. High, firm breasts flattened against his bare chest. Nipples rigid with cold peaked under the wet silk and poked into his skin. Hanging on to his professional detachment with some effort, Pete forced himself to ignore the sensations she caused in the upper portion of his body. He wasn't quite as successful with the lower portion. Each step up the stairs brought her nicely rounded bottom bumping into his groin.

He carried her into the bathroom that took up half of the loft. Relief edged with regret lanced through him when she pulled together a shaky smile.

"I...can man...age."

He lowered her feet to the thick carpet, but kept an arm around her waist while he reached into the freestanding glass-and-brass shower cubicle to twist the knobs. When steam filled the stall, he disengaged himself.

"I'll round up some dry clothes while you defrost. Call me when you're through."

Abby didn't think she'd ever be through. In fact, she seriously considered taking up permanent residence in the glass shower stall. Blessed heat swirled around it, and around her. Hot water streamed down her body to pool at her feet. For the first time since leaving the shop this morning, her toes felt as though they were still attached to the rest of her. She propped her shoulders against the sturdy glass wall, fighting the urge to just slide down and puddle on the royal blue tile for the rest of the night, if not the rest of her life.

Gradually the few seconds of stark terror she'd experienced when the van slid sideways across the icy road faded from her consciousness. So did the sickening crunch when its back end had slammed into the tree. She had no idea how much damage the Antiquemobile had sustained. At this moment, she didn't really care. She knew she could increase the amount of the small-business loan she planned to take out, just enough to cover the cost of a new van to complement her new shop. She'd think about that later, though. Right now, more important matters concerned her.

Like where she was going to find the energy to turn off the taps and step out of the shower. Pete provided the motivation some moments later by rapping on the bathroom door.

"Abby? If you're going under for the third time, I'm pretty good at mouth-to-mouth."

She smiled ruefully. Good? Judging by his kiss, she'd say he was a whole lot better than good. If she had to rate Pete O'Brian's mouth-to-mouth technique on a scale ranging from shattering to mind-bending, she'd give him one-hundred-percent erotic.

What a shame that same incredibly skilled mouth had a tendency to voice rather unflattering opinions of Beth. Sighing, she lifted her face to the pulsing stream.

Abby wasn't blind to her sister's faults, as many people seemed to think—Marissa, particularly. She just weighed them against the uncritical, unrestrained love Beth gave her. A love that had buoyed her during the bleak years after their parents' deaths. A fierce love that had kept them together every time the nameless, faceless "system" tried to separate the Davis girls.

"Abby?"

"I'll be out in a minute."

"I didn't bring much except my uniform and some exercise gear back to the States with me. I left some sweats on the bed for you. While you dress, I'll go downstairs and fix you something hot to drink."

Reaching for the white ceramic faucets, Abby cut off the life-giving warmth and stepped out of the stall. Luckily, the bathroom came equipped with a thick terry robe, a blow-dryer, and an assortment of luxurious lotions and creams. Feeling almost human again, she dried her hair, then went into the bedroom.

Two of her could have fit into the faded maroon sweats and thick socks Pete had left on the bed. The sweatshirt was emblazoned with USAF PARARESCUE in big silver letters on the back, and it hung to her knees. She rolled the maroon sweatpants up at the waist and cuffs, then pulled the warm socks on gratefully over her perennially cold feet.

Pete met her at the bottom of the staircase and handed her a steaming mug. Wrapping both palms around the footed mug, Abby sniffed at the chocolate-scented swirls rising above its rim.

"Mmm . . . this smells wonderful."

"You might try a test sip before you . . ."

His warning came too late. Abby had already blown the steam away and taken a big gulp.

Her eyes widened in shock, then filled with instant tears. She tried without success to work her paralyzed throat muscles. At her frantic, gurgling appeal, Pete thumped her on the back. Swallow by fiery swallow, the explosive brew scorched its way down her windpipe. By the time it reached her stomach, every nerve in her body was sending out distress signals.

"Wh-what's in this?"

"Hot chocolate. A little rum. The finest cognac money can buy. And several other ingredients from the well-stocked bar that you probably don't want to know about."

"Good Lord!" Tears trickling down her cheeks, Abby gaped at the innocuous-looking mug.

"The PJs have a name for this particular pick-me-up," Pete told her, grinning. "But we don't use it in mixed company."

"I'm not surprised!" She swiped the back of her hand across her eyes. "Is that what you call yourselves, you and Jordy? PJs?"

"It's an old abbreviation, for parajumpers. We're assigned to pararescue or special tactics now, but the original initials still follow us around." He gestured with his own mug. "Why don't you sit down by the fire and recover?"

"I don't think I'll ever recover."

She crossed the oak floor and sank into a love seat done in a rich blue-green-and-gold plaid. Pete took the facing love seat, his long legs angled toward the fire and a lazy smile tugging at his mouth. He'd pulled on a blue cotton shirt, she saw, and well-used running shoes that undoubtedly saw duty with the warm sweats she was now wearing. His beaver-brown hair glistened with dark lights, telling Abby that he'd taken advantage of the shower stall upstairs sometime prior to her extended occupancy.

He looked loose, and more relaxed than she'd yet seen him. And very much at home amid the luxury of oak paneling, rich fabrics and the fine handcrafted furnishings that filled the cottage. Strange, Abby mused, taking another, far more cautious sip from the steaming mug. With his rugged, uncompromising features and tough exterior, she wouldn't have imagined that he could appear so...so approachable.

And so incredibly sexy.

"I'll go down and take a look at the van in the morning," he said, breaking into her disturbing thoughts. "Maybe I can get it out of the ditch."

"Maybe. But you'll have to unwrap the back end from around a pine tree first."

"That bad, huh?"

"That bad. Oh, well, Beth's been urging me to retire the Antiquemobile for ages. I guess it's time to think about a replacement."

"That's one thing your sister and I can agree on, anyway."

Abby threw him a warning look. Wisely, he retreated to safer ground.

"Are you hungry? I started to call the kitchen and ask them to deliver that cake you promised me, but I thought I'd better wait and see if you were still up to it."

"Rum-soaked raisins on top of the PJs' special concoction? I don't think so. But I wouldn't mind a taste of the standing rib roast and Vidalia-onion soufflé I ordered for the wedding supper."

"Onion soufflé?"

The doubtful note in his voice won a chuckle from her. "Trust me. It's the chef's specialty. People come from all over the South just to experience it."

"If you say so. Hang tight. I'll call room service."

He went across the room to consult the resort directory on the desk angled beside a curtained floor-to-ceiling window. A few moments later he returned, a crease between his dark brows.

"They promised to do their best, but it'll take a while. The overflow of football fans and a number of strategic personnel absences due to the weather have taxed their resources to the limit."

Abby tucked her toes under her on the well-cushioned couch, not altogether unhappy about the delay. So she hadn't eaten anything since breakfast? So her stomach had performed a joyous leap at the mere mention of food? She wouldn't mind some time before the fire to savor her potent drink, and the even more potent male opposite her.

"In case my teeth were chattering too loudly for you to hear it before, I want to thank you again for taking me in. And for the, ah, physical exam."

His eyes glinted at her delicate reference to the way he'd stripped her of everything but her underwear and her granny boots, then run his hands over her body. Even in her wet, shaking state, Abby had seen that he knew what he was doing.

"You're welcome."

"Is that part of your job? Giving first aid, I mean."

"We can do a little better than first aid. Every PJ qualifies for national level certification as an EMT before graduating from our academy. We're also trained in arctic and jungle survival, aircrew operations and underwater egress."

"And jumping out of airplanes," she added with a grimace.

A shadow rippled across his face. Or it might have been the flickering firelight. It was gone so swiftly, she wasn't sure.

"That's part of the job," he replied evenly. "Not my favorite part, I'll admit."

"Which is?"

His shoulders relaxed under their covering of blue cotton. "Putting our chopper down beside a smoking pile of wreckage and watching a crew member run toward us, a grin plastered across his face. Or her face," he amended, with a smile at Abby. "A growing number of our air force aircrew members are women."

"Good for them!"

His smile broadened. "Right now, women are barred from participating in direct combat, which includes combat rescue. But I don't think it'll be long before the first female PJ reports for duty."

Abby knew little about the military, and nothing at all about combat rescue, but she'd heard enough about Tailhook and other scandals in the news to suspect that not all military men welcomed females in their ranks. Curious about where Pete stood on the matter, she probed further.

"Will you have a problem accepting a female PJ?"

"I've been in rescue twenty-two years. It's my life. I'll accept anyone or anything that improves our ability to perform our mission."

The quiet dignity of his reply gave Abby her first glimpse behind Pete O'Brian's impenetrable exterior.

This man was a far more complex creature than his tough-guy image suggested.

"What about you, Abigail? How long have you been into antiques?"

"How did you know I'm in the antique business?"

"Jordy told me. He also gave me your phone numbers at home and at work, in case there was a foul-up at the airport and Beth and I missed each other."

They both left unsaid just how big a foul-up occurred at the airport.

"I was going to call you tomorrow, you know," he added slowly, almost reluctantly.

Surprise and pleasure percolated through her. "No, I didn't know."

"I wanted to make sure you got home okay. Besides, I owed you a dinner, remember?"

Abby remembered. She also remembered that she'd intended to find out a bit more about him during that dinner...like his exact marital status. She nibbled on her lower lip, searching for a subtle way to find out what she wanted to know. There wasn't one, she decided, so she opted for a direct approach.

"I don't usually accept dinner invitations from men I don't know. Is there someone waiting for you in England who might object to us dining together?"

"No, I'm divorced. My wife got tired of a husband who spent more time in the air than on the ground."

Even though that was the answer she'd been looking for, Abby felt uncomfortable at having pried it out of him.

"Oh, I'm sorry."

"It happened a long time ago. Almost eight years, and I still spend more time in the air than on the ground. Too much to form the kind of relationship where anyone would be waiting for me when I got down, anyway. How about you?" he asked, neatly turning the tables. "Anyone waiting for you at home?"

His frank response deserved an equally honest answer.

"No, no one. I've been too busy with work and getting Beth through school. And with studying for my appraiser's license." She couldn't resist adding a pleased little footnote. "I got it last year."

"Okay, I admit my ignorance. What does a person do with an appraiser's license?"

"Detailed descriptions of antiques for insurance purposes, mostly. Also, I value the contents of homes and conduct sales when families need to dispose of an estate. Right now I'm working out of shop called Things Past, but I plan to open my own business."

"Your own antique business? I'm impressed."

Abby took another sip of the chocolate neutron bomb, then set it aside. Once a person knew what to expect, the drink was actually pretty palatable. Welcome warmth curled in her tummy as she drew up her legs and propped her chin on her knees.

"I've been saving every penny since Beth finished college," she confided. "And spending every weekend scouring the countryside for stock. I've got things stashed in rental storage facilities all around Atlanta."

"What kind of things?"

"*All* kinds of things. Primitives. Glassware. Jewelry. Beautiful pieces of period furniture."

"Good stuff, huh?"

Warmed by the chocolate and his interest, Abby opened up far more than she usually did. Beth didn't share her passion for all things old and well loved. Marissa did, of course, but for obvious reasons, Abby hadn't told her boss about her careful acquisitions.

"You should see the George IV four-poster bed I found in an old barn outside Macon." Her eyes lit up as she described her treasure. "It's solid mahogany. Crafted by one of the premier cabinetmakers in England. I've traced it to a bill of lading written in 1838. It was shipped to Twelve Oaks Plantation as a birthday gift for Mrs. Burgess Clement, of the Macon Clements."

"Pretty fancy pedigree."

The fervent light in Abby's cinnamon-brown eyes fascinated Pete. This was an aspect of her he hadn't yet seen. Vibrant. Glowing. Lost in the pleasure of her profession.

His fingers tightened on the ceramic mug. What would it take, he wondered, to nudge that pleasure one step further? To make it less professional? More personal?

"The bed was on Twelve Oaks' property inventory until well after the War between the States," she continued. "Mrs. Clements passed it to one of her granddaughters, who in turn passed it to one of the great-

great-granddaughters. Can you imagine all the Clement women who must have slept in that bed? Birthed their babies there? Welcomed their men home there?''

Her soft, dreamy query evoked a juxtaposition of Abby and beds that took Pete by the throat. He swallowed, hard, and set his mug aside. No more of the PJs' special concoction for him. He had enough trouble reining in his galloping fantasies as it was.

His abrupt movement drew her out of her reverie. Smiling, she brought him into the conversation. "I'll bet you've seen the inside of some beautiful manor houses in England, filled with all kinds of treasures.''

Pete had seen the inside of more pubs than manor houses, but he responded to the deep-seated need in her eyes.

"I've been to Windsor a few times. And to Stonecross Keep, which isn't far from Mildenhall, where we're stationed.''

"Really? What period is it?''

"Stonecross? Norman, I think. It's pretty solid, all square towers and stone battlements.''

"What about the inside? How is it furnished?''

Pete's mouth curved. If one of his troops had told him he'd be spending an evening discussing castle furniture with a woman who triggered some very fundamental instincts in him, he would have sent the man for a psych eval. Hoping that none of this would get ever back to Jordy, he searched his memory for details of medieval furnishings.

Either his account of black-beamed ceilings and big, square trestle tables was more boring than even he thought it would be, or the PJs' brew was more potent than Abby was used to. Halfway through his rambling discourse, her lids fluttered down. Once. Twice. The third time, they didn't quite make it back up.

Pete droned on, inventing details when his sketchy memory failed. After the shock of the accident, she could probably use a short nap until dinner arrived. He wouldn't mind resting his sandpapery eyelids for a few minutes, either.

Her jaw waggled on its perch atop her knees, then slid off. She jerked awake, embarrassment staining her cheeks. Moments later, she sagged against the couch. She was out for the count.

Moving with a stealth unaffected by his stiff knee, Pete mounted the stairs and pulled a couple of blankets from the closet at the rear of the loft. When he tucked the downy royal blue cover around Abby's shoulders, she gave a little mewl of delight and burrowed into its warmth. Her chin caught Pete's hand. Sighing, she dug a nest for it in his palm.

Smiling, he gave in to temptation and stroked the side of her jaw with his thumb. Her skin felt as silky as it looked, reminding him of the rippling, sun-warmed stream he used to fish in as a boy. Her scent drifted up to him, a mixture of shower soap and chocolate. Pete detected her soft, steady pulse under his thumb pad. His tripped into double time.

The lust he felt for Abby expanded, deepened, took on different shapes and colors. Like those in a kaleidoscope, the shapes had no meaning. The colors tumbled and changed too swiftly to have any substance. Pete felt the subtle shift, and it was all he could do not to gather her in his arms and join her on the plaid love seat.

Exercising a discretion he suspected he'd regret later, he retreated to the opposite sofa. Then he rested his head against the high back, propped his feet on the oak coffee table and gave himself up to the pleasure of watching the firelight play on Abby's face.

Minutes, or maybe hours, later, a muffled thump jerked him from a deep, exhausted sleep.

Groggy, he decided that dinner must have finally arrived. Only after he pushed himself upright did he realize that someone had turned off the heat. And the lights. An inky blackness pierced only by a dim red glow from the dying fire blanketed the entire cottage. Cold air knifed into his lungs with each breath.

Instant, instinctive wariness wiped away his grogginess. Something was wrong. Very wrong.

His gaze narrowed on the empty love seat opposite his. As swift and silent as a jungle cat, he rose to his feet. The tension that had become second nature to him in the past few weeks coiled in his gut. Like a predator seeking its prey, he searched the darkness.

She was down on one knee beside his leather carryall. Undershirts spilled onto the floor, forming vague white blurs. In the meager glow from the fire, the object she held in her hand was unmistakable. Its twisted, tortured shape had been burned into Pete's soul.

He crossed the floor in three noiseless strides. Wrapping a hard hand around her upper arm, he yanked her to her feet. She gave a startled squeak and dropped the piece of metal. It clattered on the oak flooring and lay between them like a small, lethal bomb.

Pete's fingers dug into her soft flesh. "What the hell were you doing with that?"

Four

———

Speechless with surprise, Abby stared at the man who gripped her. His face was a shadowed mask in the dim red glow of the fire, but she couldn't mistake the anger in his dark eyes.

When she didn't respond immediately, he bent, dragging her down with him, and scooped up the bit of metal.

"Answer me, dammit. What did you want with this?"

Abby found her voice, and a healthy surge of anger, as well.

"I didn't want *anything* with it. It fell out on the floor when I was digging through your underwear, and I picked it up."

"You want to tell me why you were digging through my gear?"

"You want to let go of my arm?"

They faced each other, his eyes cold and flat, hers narrowed to daggers behind a shield of thick lashes. Abby stood her ground, unflinching. The silence stretched between them like a challenge.

At last he uncurled his fingers, one by one. The apology, when it came, sounded like the scrape of broken glass.

"I'm sorry."

"You should be," she shot back, giving him a look that should have sliced six inches off him then and there. "You scared me half to death. Just what is that thing, anyway?"

His jaw squared. "A static-line retriever support."

"Oh, that tells me a lot!"

Imperceptibly the stark lines in his face eased. He rolled his shoulders, as if shifting a mountainous weight, and sidestepped her sarcastic retort.

"What were you doing in my carryall?"

"If you must know, I was looking for another pair of socks."

She was more exasperated than angry now, and a little embarrassed at having been caught rooting around in his underwear, although she wasn't about to admit it.

"My feet were cold. They *are* cold. They're freezing, as a matter of fact. Along with the rest of me. I didn't think you'd mind if I borrowed another pair of socks, since everything else I'm wearing at this moment happens to be yours. Obviously, I was wrong.''

"You're welcome to the socks."

"Thank you very much. Now, would you mind telling what the heck this little scene is all about? And then turn up the heat in this place," Abby added, rubbing her arms as a series of shivers racked her. "You may enjoy sleeping on glaciers and ice packs. I don't."

"I didn't turn off the heat," he replied, his voice almost back to its normal rumble. "Or the lights, for that matter. We must have blown a fuse. I'll go find the circuit box."

He slipped the shard of metal into his pocket and started to turn away. This time it was Abby who latched on to an arm with a tight grip.

"Oh, no, you don't. I want an answer, O'Brian. I think I deserve one, after that little display of overdone machoism. What the heck just happened here? What is that bit of metal, anyway?''

A tight almost-smile cranked up one corner of his mouth. "Machoism? Is that a word?"

"If it isn't, it should be. It's the only way to describe your behavior." She folded her arms across her sweatshirt-clad chest. "I'm waiting."

"You're also freezing," he pointed out.

His gaze skimmed down to her feet, crossed one over the other in a futile attempt to warm her ice-cold digits. As he took in her awkward, pigeon-toed stance, the remaining tension drained from his face.

"Let me get the heat and lights back on. Then I'll tell you what I can."

He'd tell her what he could? She frowned, skeptical, and now curious, as well.

When she didn't budge, he gave a faint, tired smile. "I promise."

Brows furrowed, Abby headed back to the love seat she'd vacated just moments before. Grabbing one of the blankets, she draped it around her shoulders and knelt to stir the glowing embers with the poker while Pete shrugged into his leather jacket. As she watched him head for the front door, it occurred to her that there might be more to his return to the States than the simple desire to do Jordy a favor.

She had no idea what, although she guessed it was linked to the strange object she'd found while rooting around for an extra pair of socks. Frowning, she extracted a log from the neat stack on the hearth and laid it in the grate before adding kindling to the glowing embers to rebuild a flame.

Pete returned almost immediately. Bolting the door behind him, he crossed the darkened room in his swift stride.

"It's not a blown fuse. The whole resort's dark. There isn't light showing anywhere, not even at the main lodge below us."

"You're kidding!" She peered at his shadowed face and groaned. "You're not kidding."

"'Fraid not. A main transformer must have blown. Or maybe the weather took down some power lines."

He reached for the phone on the end table. Frowning, he listened for a few seconds, then replaced the receiver.

"The phones are gone, too. I'm not surprised. It's really nasty out there. Everything's coated with ice and slick as spit."

"Oh, no! I suppose that means we won't get our dinner."

Tilting his wrist to the firelight, Pete squinted at his watch. "We didn't get our dinner four hours ago. Guess we were both too exhausted to notice."

"I'm not exhausted now," she mumbled, poking at the fire. "Just hungry."

Pete hunkered down beside her and warmed his hands at the growing blaze. "After seeing what it's like out there, my guess is we'll be lucky to get breakfast."

Until that moment, Abby had been feeling a hollow sort of emptiness. At the thought of missing out on tomorrow's breakfast, as well as tonight's onion soufflé, she went from empty to positively starving.

She rose, gathering the folds of her blanket. They both needed sustenance, and she wanted an explanation. Deciding food came first, she headed for the kitchenette tucked below the loft.

"This place has to come equipped with a stash of munchies. It's got everything else. You tend the cook fire, and I'll go hunt for food."

She found a cache in the kitchen, and another in the wet bar. Arms laden with an assortment of packages, bottles and cans, she returned to the sitting room. Welcome heat now radiated from the fire Pete had restored to full strength.

"How do cashews, Eagle brand sour-cream potato chips, red caviar and cocktail olives sound?"

"Except for the caviar, pretty darn good."

"We'll leave that for the next stranded guests, then." She dumped the packages on the coffee table and placed the cans and bottles in a neat row. "You have a choice. Imported wine, imported beer, imported mineral water or Georgia's own orange cream soda."

"I'll have whatever you're having."

Pete added another log to the now blazing fire, then rose and dusted his hands on his thighs. While Abby went back to the kitchen to search for a bottle opener, he shoved one of the facing love seats aside and swung the other around to face the fire, crowding it and the coffee table as close to the heat source as was safe.

Abby's steps slowed when she saw the new arrangement. It made more sense, of course, to share the small love seat and catch all the heat they could from the fire. But did she really want to huddle close to a man who had all but attacked her a few moments ago?

No, *attacked* was the wrong word. He'd startled her, certainly. The intensity of his third degree had jolted her, just as his grip on her arm had angered her. Still, she hadn't felt physically threatened. Not for a moment.

It came as a slight shock to Abby to realize that she trusted Pete. She'd met him only a few hours ago, yet some deep-seated feminine instinct told her he wouldn't harm her. Not intentionally, and not physically.

Emotionally, however, Senior Master Sergeant Pete O'Brian constituted a serious threat to her inner peace. Honesty compelled Abby to admit that she still hadn't quite recovered from his kiss. Or from the feel of his hands, gentle and sure on her ribs, when he'd searched for possible injuries. Yet every time she came close to liking the blasted man, he said or did something that put up her hackles—like accusing her of rifling his carryall to find a twisted scrap of metal!

Curiosity about that small, unidentifiable object overcame the doubts she harbored about Pete O'Brian's impact on her emotions. She wanted to know more about it. More about him.

She waited until they'd settled on the love seat, one blanket draped across their laps, another over their shoulders. The blazing fire sent the frosty chill in the cottage retreating to the shadows. Pete attacked the junk-food feast with hungry gusto. Abby matched him munch for munch. After they tossed a pile of empty packages aside, she dusted the potato-chip crumbs from her lap and hunched her knees under the blanket.

"I'm still waiting," she reminded him.

He didn't pretend to misunderstand. Resting his orange pop bottle on his stomach, he gave her a long, considering look.

"It's not exactly a bedtime story, Abby."

The warning raised a ripple of gooseflesh that had nothing to do with the cold. Tucking her arms under the blanket, she shifted a bit to face him.

"Tell me."

His gaze drifted to the fire. Abby sensed that he was sifting. Sorting. Deciding what he "could" tell her. He was quiet for so long, she almost prompted him again.

Something held her back. The taut cast to his face, maybe, bronzed by the firelight. Or the midnight-blue eyes that saw things she didn't in the dancing flames.

"It was a training jump," he said at last, his voice flat. "A night requal. I didn't need the canopy time, but I wanted to test our new free-fall rig."

Abby waited for him to continue, unconsciously massaging her ever-cold toes under the blanket. The small movement distracted him. He glanced down, then turned to set aside his soft drink. To her surprise, he slipped his arms under the cover and lifted her feet into his lap. His hands took up where hers had left off. Through a double layer of heavy cotton socks, Abby felt his strength. And warmth. And gentleness.

The story he told her wasn't gentle, though. It came out slowly. In measured bits. As though the horror were more manageable in small pieces.

"The others were doing static-line jumps. It was a clear night for a change, but windy. The team went out, one by one. All except Carrington. Our rookie."

His hands stilled, then resumed their slow stroking.

"The kid was nervous, despite his bravado. He checked his static line. Rechecked it. Held it in his left hand as he went out the door."

His fingers dug into her arch. Abby held her breath.

"I was right behind him."

Pete stared into the fire, seeing again the black hole of the open hatch. Feeling the cold wind slice into him. Hearing the rattle of the metal hook on the static line as Carrington went out.

"The kid didn't let go in time. His arm tangled in the line, hung him up. Then the slipstream caught him. Slammed him against the plane's belly. Hard. Then he hit again."

It was a parachutist's second-worst nightmare. A hung jumper, tethered by a thin, tensile umbilical to a plane plowing through the night skies at a hundred and thirty knots.

"He was unconscious, so we couldn't cut his static line loose. The pilot banked, trying to angle the plane so the jumpmaster could winch him in."

He's hooked! The jumpmaster's frantic shouts pounded in Pete's head. *Dammit, he's hooked on something! I can't reel him in!*

They'd worked together, he and the young sergeant. Cursing and wrenching at the static-line retriever, while Carrington slammed into the undercarriage time and again.

"Then the retriever support gave."

Pete's voice gave no hint of the panic that had sliced through him when the metal support snapped and Carrington's tether whipped out the open hatch. Pete had followed less than a second later, diving into blackness, searching for the rookie's chem lights and flashing strobe in a vast, empty hell.

"I went out after him."

He'd caught the spinning, tumbling Carrington seconds before it would have been too late for both of them.

"I yanked the cord on his reserve. It's smaller than the free-fall chute, faster. He hit the ground before me, hard. Then the wind caught him. I followed his strobe, flew into his canopy. It wasn't a pretty landing, but I stopped his drag."

The soft, indrawn hiss beside him dragged Pete back from a dark, deserted hayfield.

"Was . . . was he all right?"

"He survived, but he'll never fly again."

The doctors weren't sure he'd ever walk again, either, but the kid was determined to prove them wrong.

"The accident board examined everything. Our jump procedures. The kid's training records. They sent the static-line retriever back for stress and fatigue analysis. The findings are confidential. . . ."

His words trailed off. He shouldn't be telling her this much. Pete knew it. A military man to his bone, he believed in discipline, in rules and regulations, in making the system work.

Then his eyes locked with hers. He saw sympathy in their brown depths, and a strength that Beth must have turned to continually. Against his better judgment, Pete felt himself drawn to that same, steady strength.

"The board determined it was a freak accident, compounded by simple human error. The support shouldn't have failed, but it did. Carrington should have released his static line sooner, but he didn't. I should have seen how he gripped the line, but I didn't."

He didn't realize his fingers had frozen around Abby's foot until she tried to tug it free. He frowned down at his lap, trying to remember just how the heck her feet had ended up there in the first place. Belatedly he loosened his grip. She surged up onto her knees, dragging the blankets with her.

"Surely they don't blame you for the accident!" she exclaimed. "No one could blame you. My God, you brought him down!"

Pete blinked at the avenging goddess who knelt beside him, her hair a wild halo of disheveled curls, her brown eyes fired with indignation on his behalf. Her passion pushed the black, bleak night back into the small chamber of his mind where it would always reside.

"No, they don't blame me," he replied quietly. "I blame myself."

Shocked, she sank back on her heels. "Why?"

"I should have seen how nervous the kid was. He was still a rookie, and too damn cocky for his own good." He let out a long, slow breath. "That's why I pried that scrap of metal off the plane. Why I keep it as a reminder of what can go wrong every time I send my men on a training mission or out on an operation."

He slanted her an apologetic glance.

"I guess that's why I overreacted a while ago, too. I'm sorry."

"Apology accepted."

The reply was low, hardly more than a whisper. Pete closed the door in his mind. He wasn't looking for sympathy, and didn't want it. Abby wasn't quite ready to let go of that night, though.

"Is that what brought you back to the States?" she asked. "The accident?"

Nodding, he reached for her foot. "I bunged up my knee and am off jump status for a while. I'm scheduled to meet a medical evaluation board in San Antonio next week."

She gave a tiny sigh of pleasure when he began to knead her toes once more. "So what does a medical evaluation board do?"

"Poke and probe and run more tests."

Abby suspected there was more to this medical board than his deliberately offhand reply indicated. Surely there were doctors in England who could poke and probe and run tests. The fact that Pete had been sent back to the States held a significance she didn't understand. But before she could ask, he dragged her foot out from under the blanket and lifted it to eye level.

"Good Lord, woman, you're the first person I've ever met with Popsicles attached to her ankles."

"Now you know why I wanted those socks!"

"What do you do, put your shoes in the freezer at night to slow the circulation in your feet?"

"I've always been, er, cold-toed."

"Here, scoot over this way and put your feet to the fire."

Somehow, Abby ended up more in his lap than out of it. Some way, his arm slipped from the back of the love seat to the circle of her waist. Strangely uninclined to rectify the situation, she wiggled a bit to make herself more comfortable.

It occurred to her that they fit together perfectly. He was taller than she, and far more solid. Yet hip matched hip, and thigh nestled against thigh. Her shoulder tucked under his at just the right angle. His formed the perfect support for her head. She felt the fine hair at her temple stir with each slow, steady breath he took.

She wouldn't mind at all if the electricity stayed off a while. A good while.

When she realized the dangerous path her thoughts were taking, Abby tried to cut them off. She and Pete would only be together for a few more hours, she reminded herself sternly. Just until the sun came up and warmed the icy roads. Then she'd go back to an apartment filled with floor plans and sketches for her new shop, and he'd go back to the military that was his life.

Their chosen life-styles couldn't be more different, Abby mused. Hers centered around the need for an anchor, for stability, for the roots she craved. His involved constant movement, and the danger he'd touched on so briefly tonight.

For these few hours, though, their separate paths had merged, a tiny voice argued. For these few hours, they were together.

The small, insistent voice came from someplace deep inside Abby. Someplace she hadn't explored in a long time. Not since Derek. No, not even during Derek. She couldn't remember ever feeling this slow, insidious pleasure the first time he'd taken her in his arms.

Not that Pete had taken her in his arms, exactly. He was just…sharing her warmth. As she was sharing his.

Sure. Of course. Uh-huh. Even Beth hadn't resorted to that lame excuse during her rather tumultuous post-adolescent years. Sighing at the confused, half-formed jumble of needs Pete stirred in her, Abby snuggled against his side.

His voice rumbled against her ear. "Toes warm enough now?"

Smiling, she angled her head back. "I'm warm all over."

She hadn't intended any sort of double entendre, but of course the hidden meaning jumped out at her the moment the words were out. Embarrassment eddied through Abby, and a glint appeared in Pete's indigo eyes. For the life of her, she couldn't tell whether it was amusement, interest or regret.

"Me too," he admitted. "All over."

Abby's pulse tripped, skipped, then took off at triple speed. She might not have meant to convey a sensual message. Pete certainly did. She saw it in the way his gaze moved over her face and snagged on her mouth. Heard it in the husky note in his voice.

Abby held her breath, sure that he would follow up on that interesting remark. All he had to do was bend his head. Just an inch or two. When he didn't, disappointment prickled the surface of her skin.

"Abby?"

"Mmmm?"

"About that kiss at the airport..."

"Yes?"

"I told you I wasn't sorry."

"Yes."

"If I kiss you again, I'm afraid I might be. Very sorry. Because a kiss won't be enough this time."

He was right. The mouth hovering just inches from her own set off alarms all over her body. One kiss wouldn't be enough, she acknowledged. For either of them. Taking it any further would be crazy, though. And stupid. *Not* something that sober, sensible Abby should even contemplate, let alone indulge in.

A lifetime of caution, of shielding herself and Beth from the unintentional hurt too often caused by the strangers who passed through their lives, pulled Abby back from the brink.

"Then we'd better forgo the kiss and just enjoy the fire." She infused her reply with a deliberately light note. "We don't want you to regret what we both know would be a mistake."

His breath came out in a long, slow release. Then he nodded and settled himself more comfortably against the sofa. A slight adjustment brought Abby against his warmth.

"Too late," he murmured against her hair. "I already do."

Five

Abby woke to a world of piercing white light. It filled the cottage with dazzling brightness, and made the cold seem even sharper and more cutting.

She curled in a tight ball under the mounded blue covers, testing the air with the tip of her nose. Obviously, the electricity hadn't been restored during the night. Nor had the phone service. The receiver was off the hook on the end table, she saw, but no shrill beep sounded to advise her of that fact.

"Great," she muttered, tucking her nose back under the covers. So much for the Pines' exalted reputation. No heat. No phone service. Probably no hot water. No hot breakfast. No hot anything, except the fire blazing cheerfully in the grate.

And the memory of a night spent in Pete's arms.

That alone was enough to suffuse Abby's entire being with a wash of delicious warmth. She closed her eyes, recalling each shift of their bodies as they'd drifted into sleep. The times Pete had gotten up to feed the fire, then returned to gather her against him. His rather sonorous breathing a couple of times during the night. Her deplorable tendency to drape herself around him like plastic wrap in her sleep.

Common sense had motivated her to draw back from Pete's kiss. Her body had reacted to him on a more instinctive level, seeking warmth and comfort and a closeness that was all too physical.

His body had reacted, too.

Abby's face burned as she remembered how she'd dozed off and somehow hitched a leg up his hip. She'd come awake with a start when he gave a little grunt and tried to ease her knee from his groin. They'd both pretended not to notice the rigid protrusion her knee bumped against as it resumed its rightful place.

"Are you finally awake?"

She responded to the amused query by hunching the blankets up over her ears.

"No."

"Not ready to face the winter wonderland yet?"

She wasn't ready to face *him,* not while the memory of what her knee had encountered during its inadvertent explorations remained so vivid.

"I thought you might want to know the cottage has a gas water heater. There's enough left in the tank for a quick shower, if you want one."

Abby poked her head out of the blankets. Suddenly her layers of T-shirts and sweats and socks and blankets felt a little gamy.

"I want one."

He grinned, and the thought rocketed through Abby that any woman who wasn't severely hormonally challenged would enjoy waking up to that particular arrangement of facial features. If only it came packaged with one or two of her more basic requirements for a mate, like a cheerful acceptance of Beth, with all her exasperating faults. Or a desire to build a nest, and occasionally occupy it.

From what Pete had told her last night, the military was far more than a profession to him. It was part of his being. An essential core of training and experience that had sent him plunging through a night sky to snatch a tumbling body back from certain death. Abby couldn't see a man like Pete O'Brian needing roots, especially not the comfortable Sunday-morning-pancake-breakfast kind she craved.

"I saw more wood stacked in a shed a little way down the road," he told her. "I'll go retrieve some while you hit the showers. Then we'll decide what to do about breakfast."

The mere thought of something other than sour-cream potato chips was enough to get Abby off the love seat and up the stairs. She enjoyed roughly three and a half minutes of hot water before the pulsing stream started to run tepid. When she stepped out of the glass cubicle, instant goose bumps danced all over her skin.

Unfortunately, her black velveteen dress hadn't dried before the electricity went out last night. It was still draped over the edge of the tub where Abby had wrung it out, frozen into position. Tiny bits of ice fell off the white lace collar when she fingered it. Pete's maroon sweats, slept-in though they were, would have to do for a little while longer yet.

With the speed of an actor changing between on-stage scenes, Abby ripped off the terry robe and dived into the sweats. Sitting on the edge of the bed, she pulled on one pair of socks, then reached for another. A blur of movement outside caught her attention. Socks in hand, she rose to peer through the sliding glass doors that gave onto the balcony.

Pete was making his way down a steep slope to a shed set midway between the honeymoon cottage and its nearest neighbor, some hundred or so yards away. Traversing that sharp incline wasn't an easy task. The ground beneath his feet glittered with a layer of bright, shining crystal. Thick sleeves of glistening ice bowed the pines' branches, many of which had broken off under the crushing weight. The road leading away from the cottage gleamed like a ribbon of black coal in the sunlight. Its slick surface was no doubt why Pete had abandoned the road to work his way down the stubbled hillside.

He appeared to constitute the only living thing in this frozen, fantastic tableau. With his dark hair, brown bomber jacket and blue jeans, he stood out against the glittering background. Clutching the socks, Abby stood by the windows, watching as he slipped and slid on the treacherous slope.

Her heart jumped to her throat when he went down on one knee. His bad knee, she saw at once. Even from her elevated perspective, she couldn't miss the grimace that twisted his face. He gripped his leg just above the kneecap and pushed himself up.

"Oh, Pete!"

Her heartfelt murmur of sympathy hung on the cold air. Biting her lip, she watched him struggle to rise. Absorbed in the drama, she didn't notice the shadow coming out of the trees beside him right away. When she did, she couldn't figure out just what it was that had snared her attention.

Her first thought was that it was some kind of an animal. Something big and furry and bent over. Whatever it was, it came close to the size of a man.

Good God! Were there bears in this part of Georgia?

She jerked forward, driven by an instinctive urge to yank open the windows and alert Pete to possible danger. She had both hands on the window latch when a flash of bright color snagged her eye. Her heart pounding, she squinted through the searing glare. Then she sagged against the glass doors, feeling weak with relief and slightly idiotic.

This particular variety of Georgia bear shaved its legs and wore red ankle boots. It also appeared to be friendly. *Very* friendly, judging by the way it slipped an arm around Pete's waist and clung to him for support.

While Abby watched from above, Pete and the . . . creature started up the slope toward the cottage. Slowly. Carefully. Picking their way around pines and fallen branches. As they neared, Abby saw that the fur was reddish in color, more foxlike than bearish. From the length and stylish drape of the covering, she was willing to bet it wasn't the fake fun fur advocated by the politically correct.

Abby pulled on the second pair of socks and made her way to the front door to greet them. When she stepped onto the small porch, dazzling brightness blinded her. Flinging up a arm to shield her eyes from the glittering array of color and light, she squinted through the glare. Icy air knifed into her lungs with every breath.

Pete caught sight of her from twenty yards away and waved. It was *not* the wave of a man locked in a mortal struggle with a wild creature, Abby noted wryly.

"We've got company," he called, his breath frosting on the air. "This is Cherry. She and her husband are in the next cottage."

Abby peered at the black silk scarf wrapped around the woman's head. It covered her forehead, her nose, her mouth. It covered everything but a pair of sultry green eyes framed by impossibly long black lashes.

"Their phone and electricity are out, too," Pete reported, still panting from the climb. "Cherry saw me outside and came to see if ours was working."

The woman lifted a hand to push back her scarf. Flaming red hair spilled out, as vibrant and eye-catching as a flashing hazard signal.

"Poor Pete." She gave a husky, contralto laugh. "I practically fell into his arms when I got to him. He wasn't sure whether I was introducing myself or attacking him."

"Really?"

Abby declined to mention that she hadn't been all that sure, either. She didn't want to admit that she'd been on the verge of charging out of the cottage to rescue Pete from the clutches of a . . . Cherry.

The unwitting victim frowned as he took in her attire. "What are you doing outside without any shoes?"

"They weren't dry enough to put on yet."

"Well, you'd better get inside, before those ice cubes you call toes fall off. You and Cherry both. We decided we'd better combine forces to conserve firewood," he explained. "There's no telling how long it will take for the power to come back on."

"Oh. Good thinking."

"I'm going to go back down and tell . . ." He arched a question at the woman next to him.

"Irvin."

"I'll tell Irvin, and bring him back with me."

"Have him bring the rest of the party tray that's in the fridge," Cherry called as Pete started back down the slope, step by cautious step. "And the baguettes. Oh, and the Grey Poupon. I can't eat Danish ham without it."

Abby gave a joyous gasp. The strange feeling she'd experienced at the sight of this gorgeous, fox-furred female nestled against Pete's side evaporated.

"You have food? Real food?"

"Tons of it," Cherry replied with a friendly smile as she followed Abby inside. "You wouldn't guess it to see Irv, he's such a pipsqueak, but he chows down like a team of Clydesdales. He called ahead and made sure our cottage was well stocked before we checked in yesterday. Hey, this place is something!"

The statuesque redhead stood in the center of the room and spun in a slow circle. Her viridescent eyes gleamed as they took in the majestic proportions of the main sitting room, the soaring, beamed ceiling, the blues and greens and golds that gave richness and warmth to the oak furnishings.

"It's the honeymoon suite," Abby explained as she scooped a blanket from the love seat and draped it around her shoulders. Lifting a foot, she propped it on the hearth to toast.

"The honeymoon suite! Oh, sweetie, I'm sorry! Pete didn't tell me you were on your honeymoon." Hitching up the collar of her coat, Cherry headed for the door. "You two don't want Irv and me around while you invent new ways to keep warm."

"No, wait! We're not married. I mean, we're not on our honeymoon. That is, I'm not..."

When she stumbled to a halt, the other woman laughed and gave her a knowing wink.

"That's okay. Irvin and I aren't married, either. Well, he is. Sort of. He should have signed the divorce papers ages ago, but now he's decided he wants the Lincoln."

Abby lifted her other foot to the blaze, both amused and a bit daunted by the other woman's forthright disclosures. Shaking her fiery mane in disgust, Cherry strolled over to the hearth.

"I mean, why go to court over a four-year-old Lincoln? If they were fighting over her Jag, or the Maserati Irv bought me last year, I could see it. But a Lincoln? I ask you, does that make sense?"

Pouty red lips demanded an answer.

"Maybe it has sentimental value," Abby offered weakly.

The other woman huffed, then suddenly stilled. An arrested expression came into her vivid green eyes.

"You know," she said slowly, "you might just have something there. Irv and I almost wore out the shocks when we got caught in traffic after a Cowboys night game last year. For a little guy, he sure can . . ."

"The Cowboys?" Abby interjected hastily. "Are you from Dallas?"

"Irv has his practice there, although he was born right here in Georgia, which is why we come back for this silly game every year. I'm from nowhere in particular. What about you, sweet— Say, what's your name, anyway?"

"I'm Abby. Abby Davis."

The visitor slid her hand from her coat pocket and extended it. A chunk of amethyst the size of Rhode Island caught the morning light, sending purple lasers all through the sitting room.

"I'm Cheryl Pryoskovich, but I go by my stage name, Cherry Delight."

Abby tried. She really tried. But she couldn't quite hold back a little choke as she shook Ms. Delight's hand.

At her helpless gurgle, Cherry's infectious laughter sprang loose. "I know, I know...."

Lifting her hands, she cascaded her thick mane through her fingers. In the process, she also let her coat drape open. Abby caught a glimpse of a minuscule fire-hydrant-red skirt, and a matching sweater stretched tight across a bust that could only be termed magnificent.

"With this orange hair, it was either Cherry Delight or Tomato Toots. I never would've broken out of skin flicks with that one following me around."

While Abby digested that interesting bit of information, her guest tucked her hands back in her pockets and glanced around the cottage once more.

"So you and Pete aren't married, huh? He must have it really bad for you to put you up in style like this. What does he do, anyway?"

"He's in the air force, and he doesn't have it bad for me. We're just . . . acquaintances."

"Sure you are, sweetie," Cherry teased. "I suppose that's why you're wearing his sweatshirt? And why he was so worried about your little toesies?"

Abby had a feeling she wasn't going to win this one, but she gave it another try.

"Actually, I reserved this cottage for my sister and her fiancé. They were supposed to get married yesterday, but Beth chickened out. Then Pete showed up at the airport with the news that the groom had shipped out on a no-notice deployment."

"So you decided to stand in for the bride, and Pete played groom." Cherry waggled her auburn brows. "You lucky thing. If I didn't have Irv to play with, I wouldn't mind a few parlor games with a hunk of masculine maleness like Petie-kins, myself."

Abby gave up. She cast around in her mind for a polite topic of conversation, and had just decided there wasn't one when she heard the stomp of booted feet outside. Relief coursed through her, and curiosity about the man who held this stunning woman's affections.

Pete opened the door and stood aside. A balding, stoop-shouldered man in wire-rim glasses rushed in.

"Has it come on?" he demanded. He swiped at his glasses with a gloved hand to clear the frost and answered himself immediately. "No, I can feel it hasn't. It's freezing in here. Damn!"

Cherry had said that her...friend...was a little guy, but Abby had assumed she'd exaggerated somewhat.

She hadn't.

The top of Irv's shiny head couldn't reach the buxom redhead's chin. Padded as he was in a blue ski jacket and what looked like five or six layers of sweaters and shirts, he appeared almost as round as he was tall.

"Irv, sweetie, come meet Abby."

"In a minute. Let me try one of these outlets first. Just in case."

Her eyes widening, Abby watched him get down on hands and knees and stab a plug at a wall socket. He sat back, fumbling inside his jacket for a moment, then pulled out a five-inch TV set and held it a few inches away from his nose.

"Nothing! Damn!"

"Irv..."

"Hang on a minute. I want to try another plug."

Scrambling along the oak floor on all fours, he tried the next outlet. Then the next.

Abby swung her incredulous gaze back to Pete. Grinning, he deposited a bulging pillowcase on the coffee table.

"Irv was hoping we might have juice coming in from a separate line. Just enough to get the game."

Good Lord! Abby had forgotten all about the game. The big Thanksgiving shoot-out. This was also the day a good part of the nation would sit down to a mouth-watering feast of turkey and dressing. Sweet-potato pie topped with pecans and little marshmallows. Green peas and rolls dripping with butter.

She eyed the bulging pillowcase on the coffee table with a combination of hope and resignation.

"It's bad enough the Pines didn't sand the roads so we could get out of here and make it to the stadium," Irv complained as he got to his feet. "There's no excuse for this extended power outage. Anderson's going to hear about it, that's for sure."

"Walt Anderson's chairman of the corporation that owns the Pines," Cherry explained in an aside to Abby. "Along with a string of other resorts. Irv does his gums, you know."

"Uh, no, I didn't."

Cherry beamed with pride. "Irvin's the best periodontist in Dallas."

Her proud smile folded into a sigh as she observed her companion's glum face.

"Poor baby. He's been calling a local radio station every half hour on his cellular phone to check on the roads. Now he's conserving the battery, so he can get updates on the score when the game starts. Assuming it starts at all, of course."

Irv shoved his glasses up the bridge of his nose with a stubby finger. "Of course it will. With millions in advertising riding on every minute of airtime, it has to. But we won't be there to see it." His pale blue eyes filled with despair. "I'm sorry, Cherub."

Cherub?

Once more Abby's startled gaze flew to Pete's. The laughter in them warmed her all the way down to her chilled toes. Cherry must have shared some of her artless confidences with him during their walk up the slope. Either that, or he'd figured out all by himself that angels didn't customarily robe themselves in cardinal-colored ankle boots, thigh-skimming skirts and tight sweaters. Nor did they tuck their...friends'...heads against their bosoms and plant wet little kisses all over their shiny crowns.

"Forget about the game, honey. If we miss it, we miss it. Now come meet Abby."

While Cherry performed the introductions, Pete restored the love seats to their original facing positions before the fire. The guests claimed one, leaving the other for Pete and Abby. The thought of once again sharing that yard or so of soft, well-cushioned space with the man now hunkered down before the fire, his muscled thighs straining against his jeans as he fed the blaze, sent anticipation singing through Abby's blood. With some effort, she repressed the unexpected sensation.

"Shall we eat here, close to the fire?"

"Oooh, let's!" Cherry exclaimed. "We'll have a picnic."

While Abby rooted around in the kitchenette for silverware and plates, Cherry found a linen tablecloth in a drawer and spread it over the coffee table. She then dug into the pillowcase, removing all kinds of goodies. At her suggestion, Pete unbent a hanger and used it to toast the baguettes. Irv spent his time jiggling the batteries in his TV, in the futile hope they might yet yield some power.

When the impromptu brunch was all laid out, Abby had to admit that, while it wasn't quite the elegant

Thanksgiving feast the Pines had promised its guests, it would do. It would do nicely. Silver utensils gleamed. Crystal bar glasses sparkled. And the variety of delights arrayed on the snowy linen tablecloth made her wrap an arm across her stomach to keep it from yowling.

In addition to smoked Danish ham, Irv's party tray had yielded generous helpings of sliced turkey breast and cold roast beef. It also provided crunchy carrot sticks, celery stalks, smoked oysters, and an assortment of cheeses to complement the toasted French bread. Abby had added their contribution, which included what was left of the cashews, another full jar of olives, cocktail onions, the untouched caviar, orange cream soda and a bottle of champagne.

Cherry shuddered and passed on the soda, but declared the champagne "primo." Smiling, Pete topped off her glass and filled one for Irv. Then he draped a casual arm along the back of the love seat and offered a toast with the orange soda he and Abby had opted to share.

"Here's to old traditions, and new friends."

"To *good* friends," Cherry amended with her raspy laugh, lifting her champagne flute. She nudged Irv, who sighed and raised his, as well.

"Here's to the Bulldogs, who we won't be able to watch."

Their glances swung to Abby. She hesitated, all too conscious of Pete's arm behind her and the strangers across from her. She thought of her sister, somewhere between Paris and Cairo, and felt a tiny, familiar ache.

Holidays didn't tug at Beth's emotions as deeply as they did Abby's. She'd been so much younger when their parents died. Now, she barely remembered them. She didn't seem to miss being part of a family unit as much as her older sister did...especially during the holiday season.

In contrast, Abby felt their lack of roots most keenly at this particular time of year. Over time, Thanksgiving had evolved into her least favorite celebration. Even more than Christmas, it centered around hearth and home and family, the family she and Beth didn't have. Yet as she lifted her crystal goblet of cream soda and looked into Pete's dark blue eyes, she knew that this particular Thanksgiving would hold a special place in her memories. Memories she could bring out and savor long after he'd returned to England.

Her gaze shifted to Cherry, who'd good-naturedly shared more of herself in a half hour of acquaintance than many would in a lifetime. And to Irv, his eyes glum behind the glasses, a distracted smile sketched across his face.

As families gatherings went, this one didn't quite match the picture she always carried in her heart. But, like the makeshift feast, it would do. It would do nicely.

Smiling, Abby offered a toast.

"To us."

Six

Pete tipped his glass to Abby's, then brought it to his lips. To his surprise and vague disgust, he couldn't swallow. His throat had closed with the thunderous urge to kiss the mouth so close to his own.

He'd been fighting the same damn urge since the moment he'd drifted out of sleep early this morning and found Abby sprawled across his chest. The erotic, unconscious massage her knee had given him during the night had been torture enough. Waking up to the feel of her breasts flattened against him, her chin hooked in his collarbone and her breath moist on his neck had almost sent him over the edge.

The smile in her eyes at this moment had exactly the same effect on him. Heat rose under his skin. His hands curled with the need to reach for her. His body hardened. Painfully.

Sweating under his leather jacket, Pete set his glass aside. While the others chattered and filled their plates, he tried to deal with the intensity of the desire that built in him with every hour he spent in Abby's company. This growing, gut-tightening attraction was one of the reasons he'd invited the other couple to join them. He knew he wouldn't lose control and jump Abby's unsuspecting bones in a fit of passion, but a little distraction sure as hell wouldn't hurt.

Only he wasn't distracted. If anything, the presence of the others gave him a freedom to sit back and participate lazily in the free-flowing conversation, while he drank in the sight and the scent of the woman next to him.

Still fresh from her shower, she glowed with a natural beauty that Cherry, for all her stunning presence, didn't come close to. Her hair flowed over Pete's arm, a warm, living mass of tumbled curls. When she laughed at one of Cherry's more provocative attempts to distract Irv from his unhappiness about the game, the sound sent a spear of pleasure arrowing into Pete.

Careful, O'Brian. Go real careful here.

The warning came swift and silent and almost too late. Pete recognized that fact, and slowly withdrew his arm.

Dammit, he shouldn't be sitting here wondering how he could convince Abby to extend her stay at the Pines for the rest of the holiday weekend. He shouldn't be thinking up ways to get another shot at the kiss they'd both yanked back from last night. A woman with a yearning for a bed that could be passed to her great-great-granddaughter deserved more than Pete could give her.

More than he could give her right now, anyway.

Not for the first time since the accident, Pete found himself thinking about what came after his career. When he hung up his uniform for the last time, where would he be? What would he do with the rest of his life?

The questions lay, hazy and unanswered, at the back of his mind as brunch gave way to the kind of idle conversation that turns strangers into acquaintances, then to the shared laughter that leads to friendship. Abby's charm and Cherry's earthy, irrepressible humor more than made up for Irv's distraction and repeated calls to a local radio station on his cellular phone to check the progress on the roads and the power.

"The ice storm didn't do as much damage in the city as it did here," he relayed gloomily. "Atlanta's roads are already clearing. The game's supposed to start on schedule."

"Oh, sweetie, I'm sorry." Cherry slid her hand inside his jacket and bent down to nibble on his ear. "I'll make it up to you later, I promise."

Pete felt a stirring at his side. Glancing down, he saw Abby shift and look away from the other couple. She studied the dazzling white light outside the windows. The beams high overhead. The logs stacked beside the fire. When her roving gaze came full circle and snared

Pete's, the dancing laughter in her eyes almost did him in.

The laughter yanked at him like a harness strap. That, and the complete lack of condemnation or censure. For all her refined air and ladylike manners, Abby was no prude. It hadn't taken Pete more than a few moments to recognize that Cherry was a graduate of the kinds of clubs the military authorities often declared off-limits. Abby couldn't have failed to recognize it, either. Yet she'd welcomed their unexpected guests with a cheerful smile and an unfeigned warmth.

Even now, with Cherry's hand drifting toward dangerous territory and Irv about to melt into a bald puddle on the opposite love seat, Abby displayed no embarrassment or disgust. Only that warm, gleaming laughter that drew Pete in over his head. Way over his head.

At that moment, his mental composite of Abigail Davis blurred, changed focus, reshaped itself. What emerged was a portrait of a woman. Not his admittedly male stereotype of a lady. A generous, vital woman. One he wanted with a hunger that hit him like a fist to the solar plexus.

He came within a breath of suggesting that Cherry and Irv retire to their own cottage and leave him free to nibble on Abby's ear... and her neck... and all parts south.

Luckily—or unluckily—Cherry chose that moment to plant a smacking kiss on Irv's cheek and pick up the conversation where it had been interrupted.

"So what are you going to call this shop of yours, Abby?"

"The Painted Door. I've found a wonderful old house in a part of Atlanta that's just coming back to its full glory. The house needs some work, not the least of which is sanding and refinishing the magnificent old pier-glass doors. I'm going to do that myself. I know just the color of antique green I want."

She wrapped her arms around her knees. The glowing animation that had fascinated Pete last night crept back.

"I plan to use the downstairs as a showcase for the antiques I've collected over the years. I'll live upstairs, until I get the place up and running, at least."

"Hey, maybe Irv and I can come for your grand opening. We're in Atlanta a lot. He's a guest lecturer at the university's school of dentistry." Cherry knuckled his shining scalp affectionately. "Tell them about that talk you gave on gingivitis, sweetie."

Under her good-natured prodding, Irv shucked some of his despondency over the game. It soon became apparent that a dry wit and a self-deprecating sense of humor lurked under the dentist's unprepossessing exterior. To Pete's surprise, he actually managed to hold his audience's interest in the unlikely subject. Neither Pete nor Abby objected, however, when the conversation once again ranged onto more general topics.

It had reached the lazy, wandering stage when a knock sounded on the door some time later. Pete answered it, with Irv crowding at his heels.

A weary-looking man in blue coveralls embroidered with the Pines' logo leaned a forearm against the doorframe. "Mr. O'Brian?"

"Yes."

"I'm Orlie Taggert, chief of maintenance here at the Pines. We're doing a check of the cottages. Everyone okay here?"

"We're fine. Dr. Mitchell and his party are here with us."

Relief creased Taggert's tired face. "Good. We stopped by their cottage and were worried when we didn't get an answer."

Irv nudged Pete aside, his face alight with hope. "Are the roads clear?"

"Not all of them. The county just isn't prepared to handle freak weather like this. I expect this is one of those storms folk will be talking 'bout ten, twenty years from now."

"But you made it up here."

"Had a time doing it, I'll tell you. We took a ton or so of sand out of the traps on the golf course and layered it heavy over the ice. Without that, we wouldn't have made it. The county folks are doin' their best, though. Shouldn't be too long now."

Irv's face fell. "Any idea how long it'll be before we get electricity, at least?"

Taggert hooked a thumb toward the golf cart on the pathway outside the cottage.

"I've got a crew from the power company with me. They say the lines from the substation that feeds the resort are down. We're going up there now to check it out. It's on the ridge, right behind this cottage. Can't say as I can estimate how long it'll take to fix whatever's wrong, but we'll do our best.''

The prospect of restored power and sanded roads destroyed Irv's ability to concentrate on anything except his chances of making it to the game. He checked his watch repeatedly, and squinted out the window at the crew working their way on foot up the slope behind the cottage. When the climbers reached the crest of the ridge, Irv reported on their progress with glee.

''I'm going to get a report on the roads,'' he announced, flipping open his cellular phone. ''I bet the situation's not as bad as ol' Orlie thought.''

While he paced the floor, the phone glued to his ear, Cherry rose and reached for the plates.

''Guess we could clean up a bit.'' Her mouth curved in a mischievous grin. ''Looks like Irv and I will be able to leave you two to your honeymooning soon.''

''Sooner than you think,'' Irv crowed before Pete could come up with an answer. ''The announcer says the sheriff's department reported some traffic movement on the state road.''

Abby slid her toes out of Pete's hold and got up to help Cherry.

He should be relieved, Pete told himself. He shouldn't feel this ridiculous sense of impending loss. Dammit, if he spent much longer in this enforced intimacy with Abby, he wouldn't be able to keep his hands on just her feet.

Frowning, he began stacking the crystal glasses and carried them to the kitchenette. For some time, the only sound in the cottage was the chink of plates and glasses. Then the lamp beside the coffee table flickered on, and Irv gave a whoop of joy.

"They did it! Hot damn, they did it! Come on, Cherry. Let's get back to our cottage and get ready to leave for the game. With luck, we can still make the second half."

He tucked his mobile phone into his pocket and snatched up Cherry's coat.

"It was nice meeting you both," he got out in a rush, dumping the fox fur over her shoulders. "If you're ever in Dallas, give me a call. Or if you need some periodontal work, I can recommend a good gum specialist in your area. Come on, honey. Let's hustle."

"Irv! At least let me say goodbye." Smiling, Cherry offered Abby her hand. "The Painted Door, right? I'll come by next time we're in Atlanta. I don't know anything about antiques, but I do know my condo could use some classing up."

Abby returned her warm smile. "It'll be nice to see you again."

"Come on, baby. Let's move."

After a hurried goodbye to Pete, the Junoesque redhead let Irv drag her out the front door. With their departure, silence settled over the cottage, an empty silence that slowly took on a charged tension.

Abby glanced around the room, then back at Pete. He saw in her eyes the awareness that she would leave soon, too. With the restoration of electrical power, it probably wouldn't be long until phone service followed. She could make arrangements with her road service for the van and be on her way.

Pete almost asked her to stay.

He might have, if the lights hadn't flickered and gone off. A second later, they came on again, barely noticeable in the bright sunlight streaming through the windows. A faint hum sounded. The heating unit, he guessed. The sound tore at him.

Dammit, he wanted her to stay. Correction—he wanted *her*.

More than he could remember wanting anything in a long time. He searched her eyes for some clue that she wanted him, too.

He found it an instant before the explosion rattled the windows and rocked the cottage on its foundations.

Screeching, Abby flew into his hold.

Without thinking, Pete convulsed his arms around her, protecting her body with his. Percussion waves rolled through the air, hammering at his eardrums.

They were still reverberating when the front door burst open. A white-faced Irv rushed in, Cherry a half pace behind.

"Did you hear that?" he shrilled. "We saw it! The explosion, I mean. Up on the hill behind your cottage. There was a big flash, and now blue sparks are jumping all over the place."

Pushing Abby out of his arms, Pete flowed into action.

"It must be the maintenance crew. Irv, give Cherry your cellular phone, grab some blankets and come with me. Cherry, call 911 and tell them about the explosion. We'll apprise them of the exact situation as soon as we arrive on scene. Abby, find whatever you can in the way of first aid supplies, then you both follow us up the hill. Move, people, move!"

Abby had once heard that disasters caused people to suspend emotion and act on pure instinct. She soon discovered the truth of that statement.

Before she had time to fully grasp what had happened, Pete and Irv had disappeared out the door. Moments later, she and Cherry tore out after them and started up the hill. Panting and scrabbling for purchase on the icy stubble, they half pushed, half pulled each other up the slope.

As they neared the crest, Abby's heart pounded with fear, and a growing dread of what they might find at the top. She could hear a snapping, sizzling sound, like sparks hitting water. A moan carried down to her, audible above her own rasping breath.

Her stomach clenched into a tight, quivering knot when she stumbled into a flat clearing atop the ridge. Just yards away was the entrance to a fenced enclosure housing several gray electrical boxes. The boxes huddled under a tall cranelike structure that trailed several loose wires. One thick wire undulated wildly, spitting traces of blue fire.

Horrified, Abby saw two men lying on the ground beside the boxes. Another stumbled around outside the enclosure, dazed, his clothing smoldering.

"Stay back!" Pete shouted. "Don't touch the fence or get near that wire!"

Dumping the blankets on the ground, Irv started toward the injured man. Pete yanked him back.

"If he's walking, he's alive."

"But—"

"In an electrical situation, the rules of triage are reversed. Ignore the wounded. Go for the dead. A little CPR can bring them back."

Irv swallowed, his face now ashen. "I haven't done CPR since dental school."

"I just took a refresher course at the Y," Abby panted. "I can help."

Pete eyed the snapping, dancing line. "Okay, when the wire whips up and away, I'll go in low and drag one out. You two start on him while I go after the other. Cherry, tell 911 we have two down, one walking. Tell them we'll need burn kits and—"

He broke off and darted into the enclosure, bent almost double. Abby didn't move, didn't breathe, didn't feel her nails gouging into her palms. Even with his bad knee, Pete moved fast, so fast the lump of terror lodged in her throat didn't have time to burst out.

He was back seconds later, dragging the victim with him. Abby went down on her knees and tilted the man's head back to clear his airways.

"Oh, God!" Irv exclaimed. "It's Orlie!"

The dentist dropped to his side and ripped open the maintenance man's jacket, using two fingers to find the exact spot under his sternum to apply pressure. Crossing one fist on top of the other, he hunched his shoulders and applied pressure.

Abby counted every push. "Fifteen one, fifteen two..."

After the fifth push, she bent and breathed into Orlie's open mouth. Then she rocked back out of Irv's way, dragged air into her lungs and started counting again.

"Fifteen-one, fifteen-two..."

Afterward, Abby could never believe that she'd counted and breathed and counted and breathed for only eight or ten minutes. It seemed like hours. Weeks. Years.

She saw Pete bring the second man out and start CPR on him. She heard Cherry call in a report over the cellular phone, then take off after the dazed, stumbling third victim. Draping her fur around his shivering form, Cherry guided him over to the makeshift triage center.

Pete spared him a glance, never ceasing his steady pumping rhythm. "Keep him warm, but...don't touch the burns...on his hands or face."

By the time Abby heard the distant sound of a helicopter, she'd lost all track of time, of space, of everything but the man on the ground. The violent wash of rotor blades as the chopper skimmed the treetops just above the clearing barely penetrated her fierce concentration. She counted aloud. And breathed. And counted aloud. And breathed.

Once she thought she felt a tremor in the flaccid throat muscles under her hand. Irv must have felt something, too.

"Come on, Orlie!" he shouted, pumping on the man's chest. "Breathe, damn it! Breathe!"

Abby was so absorbed in the life-and-death drama that she gave a little scream when hands closed around her shoulder and yanked her back.

"We've got him, ma'am. We've got him."

A hulking figure took her place beside the downed man. A warm coat dropped over her shoulders. A shaking Irv came to stand beside her. Cherry joined them moments later. They huddled together, watching, praying.

Relieved by a team of rescue personnel, Pete dragged himself to his feet. Unlike the others, though, he stayed at the center of the operation. The crew recognized his expertise, Abby saw. Responded to his authority.

Another helicopter landed in the road beside their cottage. Several helmeted men appeared in the clearing soon afterward. A siren wailed in the distance. The screen of rescuers surrounding the downed men shifted, allowing Abby a glimpse of the man Pete had worked on.

"He's sitting up!" Cherry gasped.

Abby's heart gave a thump of joy so great it hurt. The exhilaration lasted all of two or three seconds. Just long enough to recognize that Orlie still lay flat on his back, unmoving.

Radios cackled. More equipment appeared. Someone shouted that they had the power company's chief engineer on the line. Pete took the radio, gave a terse description of the disaster. Moments later, the snapping, whipping line jerked upward, then suddenly went dead.

The sizzling had barely ceased when a rawboned woman in a plaid hunting jacket and a yellow helmet came panting up the slope. The senior fireman on-scene turned to greet her.

"You got here fast, Mayor. You and the rest of the disaster response team. But the situation's under control, thanks to O'Brian here."

"What about the injured?"

Abby clutched Irv's arm with tight fists as she waited for the fireman's response.

"They're all right. They got a little crisped around the edges, though, so we're going to take 'em to County General."

"Thank God."

Silently Abby echoed the mayor's heartfelt prayer.

The fireman glanced at the stretchers being loaded onto the chopper. "I don't mind tellin' you, though, two of those boys wouldn't have made it if Mr. O'Brian here hadn't known what the hell he was about."

Tipping a finger to his hat, he went off to supervise the evacuation. The mayor tucked a whisp of iron-gray hair behind her ear and tilted Pete a sharp look.

"Where'd you get your training, Mr. O'Brian?"

"In the air force. It's what I do."

"From what I can see, you do it damn well. If you ever decide you want to turn civilian, you come see me, you hear? Pineville's not much more than a village, but we sure could use someone with your kind of background on the county staff."

"I wasn't the only one who responded," Pete replied, his smile encompassing the group still huddled together a few paces away. "You should be thanking Miss Davis and Dr.—"

"Miss Davis?" The mayor jerked around, her lively black eyes snapping from Abby to Cherry. "Is one of you the Miss Davis that's staying at the Pines?"

Abby nodded. "I am."

"I'm Doretta Calvin."

At Abby's blank look, the older woman smiled. "I'm the local JP, as well as the mayor of Pineville. I was supposed to preside over your marriage ceremony last night, but the cold burst the damn pipes in the town hall. I tried to get here after that little disaster, but by then the roads had iced over."

"Oh, no! The assistant manager didn't call you?"

"No, nobody called me." She peered at Abby, then at Irv. "Hey, it's not too late, you two. If you've got the license, I'd be happy to say the words while I'm here."

Belatedly Abby realized she still had both hands dug into Irv's arm. He tugged free of her hold, his eyes widening.

"No, no..." he stuttered. "You've got the wrong groom."

"I'll say," Cherry murmured with a low, throaty chuckle.

"And the wrong bride," Abby added.

"You didn't request the services of a JP?"

"Yes, I did, but not for me. For my sister."

"Your sister?" The mayor glanced around the still-crowded site. "Is she here?"

"No, she, ah...didn't make it to the Pines this weekend."

"Didn't make it to her own wedding?" The mayor's gray brows arched, and then her sharp gaze shifted to Pete. "Are you the groom, O'Brian?"

"No, he didn't make it, either."

Mayor Calvin rocked back on her heels, her weathered face creasing into a grin. "Not much of a wedding, was it? No bride, no groom, no justice of the peace."

Abby's accumulated tension eased into a smile. "No wedding supper. No electricity or heat in what was supposed to be the honeymoon cottage."

"And no game," Irv put in glumly.

Seven

An hour later, Abby stood on the porch of the cottage beside Pete. A single thought drummed through her.

She should leave.

She should go inside, gather her things and leave.

Her common sense told her it was time to return to Atlanta and to her nice, quiet life. The past twenty-four hours had provided enough drama and nerve-twisting tension to last her a long, long time. Yet sober, sensible Abby lingered long after she should have left.

She'd waited at the accident site while a police officer took statements and another crew worked to restore power. A short while later, she'd bidden goodbye to the mayor and her team, then forced a smile at Irv's jubilant announcement that the state roads were open.

When the heat and lights came back on throughout the resort, she'd cleaned up and changed out of the faithful maroon sweats.

Now she stood beside Pete, waving goodbye to Cherry and a beaming Irv as they drove off in the resort's limousine. A wrecker followed a short distance behind the limo, towing a sadly dented Antiquemobile. The Pines' grateful manager saw both vehicles off, then walked back to the porch.

"We'll take care of your van, Miss Davis," he assured her once more.

Shoulders hunched against the cold, the aristocratic-looking innkeeper wore the marks of worry and relief on his face, but he still carried himself with the dignity of his position.

"Please, keep the rental car until your van is repaired. We'll deliver it to you in Atlanta as soon as it's ready. Are you sure we can't do anything else for you?"

"No, thank you. You've been most generous."

More than generous, in fact. He'd already told her there'd be no charge for any of the costs associated with the canceled wedding. What was more, he'd invited her and Pete to stay at the resort as guests of the management for as long as they wished, separately or together.

It was the *together* part that held Abby at the Pines.

The word triggered a fierce need within her, one she only half understood. An urgent demand that went beyond the physical. Beyond sexual. It hummed in her veins and kept her fingers clenched around the keys to the rental car the manager had presented to her. The man beside her remained silent, but Abby felt him with every tingling sense as she tried to focus on the manager's face.

"It's the least we can do," he told her. "Orlie Taggert has been with the Pines for twenty-seven years. Thanks to you, he'll be with us another twenty-seven, God willing."

"Not just me."

"No, no, of course not. Dr. Mitchell and Miss, er, Delight will always be welcome here. And Sergeant O'Brian..."

He held out his hand to Pete.

"I hope you consider the Pines your home whenever you're in this part of the country."

The utterly sincere comment spiked the strange feelings inside Abby. They leapt in her chest. Grabbed at her heart. Neither she nor the manager had any idea when Pete might be back in this part of the country. She fisted her hand around the keys. Their sharp edges cut into her palm.

She was still clutching them when the manager drove off in one of the Pines's distinctive golf carts. Unfolding her fist, she slipped the keys into the pocket of her cloak and went inside.

Pete followed, then leaned his shoulders against the door. His stance was easy, but questions shimmered in his dark blue eyes. The same questions she kept asking herself.

What was she doing?

Why had she stayed?

What did she want of him?

Abby didn't have any answers, either for herself or for him. She couldn't describe what held her. She only knew she didn't want to leave. Not now. Not yet.

She wet her lips. "You were spectacular up there, on the ridge."

"You were pretty spectacular yourself. When did you learn CPR?"

"I took a course at the Y years ago, when I got legal custody of Beth. I go for refresher training every couple of years."

"Smart lady."

They were dancing around the strange tension that gripped them. Abby knew it, but Pete was the one who acknowledged it.

Pushing his shoulders off the door, he closed the short distance between them and brought his hand up to cup her chin. A thumb traced along her cheek.

"It's okay, Abby. I understand what you're feeling."

"You do?"

"I feel it, too. A sort of high. A fierce satisfaction that won't go away."

That was true... to an extent. In those tense moments on the ridge, she'd shared some of the drama that routinely characterized Pete's life. Now she was experiencing some of the aftereffects of that adrenaline surge. She did feel the fierce satisfaction he'd described. A high she didn't want to let go of.

As she absorbed the feather-light stroke of Pete's thumb against her cheek, however, Abby acknowledged that the tremors running through her were more than just aftershocks. Far more. They went deeper, took on a more personal slant.

Unlike Pete, however, she didn't claim to understand her hazy, whirling emotions. Understanding could come later, she decided. Thinking would come later. Right now, she wanted more than the touch of his hand on her cheek.

His mouth curved in an understanding smile. "After a successful mission, we always feel the need to celebrate. To reaffirm life, I guess."

Her heart thudding, she took her courage in hand.

"How do you think we should celebrate?"

His smile moved from his lips to his eyes. "I can think of all kinds of ways to celebrate with you, Abigail, but none we wouldn't regret even more than the kiss we passed on last night."

He wasn't making this easy on her, she thought with an inner groan.

"I've been thinking about that kiss," she told him.

"Me too. A lot."

"I'm not so sure now it would have been a mistake."

His thumb stilled. Abby's blood began to pulse with a heat that had nothing to do with the restored electrical power or the mohair lining of her cloak.

"I don't want either of us to leave here with regrets, Abby."

She saw the hunger in his eyes, and felt a thrill of response deep in her belly.

"My only regret," she replied on a puff of need, "is that we're talking about it so much."

Turning her head, she brought her mouth against his palm. Her lashes fluttered down as she savored the contact with his flesh. It warmed under the wash of her breath, and bathed her face in heat. She pressed a soft kiss into the center of his palm, then another against the mound of his thumb. Her mouth moved to his fingers, her lips dragging against the pull of his skin. Her hand came up and folded over his, trapping it while she explored the rough hills and shallow valleys.

Pete didn't move. Hardly breathed. He'd never felt anything so erotic in his life as the whisper of heat from Abby's lips...until her tongue dipped into the hollow of his palm.

At the touch of her tongue on his skin, every nerve in his arm jumped. He knew he should pull his hand away. He told himself he should call a halt to this loveplay before it stopped being play.

He understood what was driving her. The same exultation sang in his veins, all mixed up with the physical attraction that had been building inside him from the moment he first laid eyes on her. It was a dangerous, combustible combination, and it fast carried him to the flash point.

"Abby. Sweetheart."

The words were a plea, and a warning.

"It's okay," she murmured against his palm. "I don't bite. Not very hard, anyway."

As if to prove her point, she nipped the mound of flesh at the base of his thumb. Then she soothed the sting with a slow, wet stroke of her tongue.

He wanted her. Pete had never wanted anything in his life as much as he wanted to bury himself in this woman's soft, slick flesh.

She wanted him, as well. He'd seen it in her eyes just before the explosion. He felt it now in the slow, seductive movement of her mouth and the velvety rasp of her tongue against his hand.

He looked down at her, imprinting the sweep of her dark lashes against her cheek in his memory bank. His hungry gaze detailed the curve of her neck. The unruly, gold-streaked hair she'd tamed into some kind of a loose braid. The prim white lace collar on her dress peeking out of the loose cloak.

This was the Abby he'd first met at the airport. This delicate, elegant creature. Then she'd struck him as the kind of woman who would expect more from a man than a fun weekend. Now, Pete realized with a tight ache, he wanted to give her more.

He couldn't give her the permanence she craved, though, and that stark, undeniable fact held him rigidly in check. He didn't know where he'd be next month, let alone next year. He'd lost one woman to the demands of his career. He didn't want to lose another.

She wasn't asking for evermores, a voice within him snarled. She wasn't asking for anything. Instead, she was giving him a slow, hot pleasure that drove everything else out of his mind.

Suddenly, without warning, the touch of her lips on his hand wasn't enough. For either of them.

Pete couldn't tell whether he jerked his hand away first or Abby lifted her head. However the shift occurred, it freed her mouth for his.

She arched into his kiss, fitting herself against him eagerly. Her arms slid free of her cloak and wrapped around his neck. Her hunger slammed into him with the force of a canopy snapping open after a long, spiraling free-fall. He dug his hands through her hair, framing her face, taking everything her mouth offered.

He had no idea how long he held her mouth captive, or when his hands left her hair. He only knew that the tight ache in his groin had expanded to a fierce, driving demand when he stripped off her voluminous cape and went to work on the buttons on the front of her dress. Moments later, it puddled at her feet.

"That's the second time you've peeled off my clothes in the middle of the sitting room," Abby said, a little breathlessly. "At least this time the heat's on."

Pete grinned. "That it is, sweetheart."

Her choke of laughter shattered his restraint. He yanked at the zipper on his jacket. Seconds later, it joined the pile on the floor. His hands speared around her waist. Curling his fingers into her black silk teddy, he pulled her against him.

"You have no idea how crazy this thing you're wearing made me the first time I saw it."

"Really?"

His hands slid up her back, then around to her front. "Really."

Lips parted, she quivered under his touch. Tight nipples budded against the black covering, and Pete sucked in a swift, stabbing breath.

"I know it isn't a George III four-poster that came over on the *Mayflower*," he growled, sweeping her into his arms, "but I've been fantasizing about you in the bed upstairs since the moment I saw it."

"George IV," Abby panted, hooking her arms around his neck. "It's George IV. And I had a few fantasies myself."

Pete attacked the stairs, not sure he could make it all the way to the loft with her breath hot in his ear and her teeth nipping at his lobe.

He did. Barely.

They tumbled to the bed together. Panting, laughing, tugging, they stripped each other of all but her panties and one of his socks. Bodies pressed together at every possible pressure point, they rolled across the bed. Greedily, he took what her mouth offered. Eagerly, she explored him with her hands and teeth and tongue. Rock-hard and hungry, Pete hooked his hands around her waist and lifted her up. His mouth closed over the tantalizing flesh of her breast.

Abby propped her hands on his shoulders, gasping when he took the aching nipple in his teeth. She'd expected her need to erupt with cataclysmic force as he nipped and teased and suckled, but she'd underestimated by several seismic degrees the total impact on her system. Fiery, volcanic heat rushed from her breast to her belly, and liquid pleasure flowed like lava from there to every nerve center in her body.

She writhed on top of him and under him, groping, stroking, returning the pleasure he gave her. Their bodies slicked, inside and out. Her hips rocked into his. A rough-haired leg scraped against her inner thigh. Somehow, in the melee of searching hands and tangled limbs, she lost her panties and he lost his other sock.

His fingers probed her wet center to prepare her. Then, without warning, he levered himself up and rolled off the bed.

"Pete... What?"

"We need protection."

It took a moment for Abby to grasp his meaning. "I... I don't have any."

"I don't, either..."

"Oh, noooo!"

His eyes danced at her anguished wail. "But I know where I can get some. Hang tight."

As if she could do anything else!

He trotted to the bathroom, and Abby pushed herself up on one elbow. Her heavy-lidded eyes cataloged a well-muscled back, a trim waist, and a world-class set of buns. She was still dealing with the impact of his tight, neat buttocks on her overheated respiratory system when he returned, a selection of brightly colored packets fanned out in his fist like a deck of cards.

"When the Pines advertises a honeymoon cottage equipped with all the amenities, they mean *all* the amenities."

The reminder that they occupied the honeymoon suite stirred a small, stray longing in one corner of Abby's heart. Resolutely she banished it. She hadn't asked Pete for any promises, and certainly didn't expect any. Ever practical, always realistic, she knew that tomorrow would take care of itself. Tonight, all she asked for was the feel of his arms around her and the thrust of his body into hers.

Lifting a brow, she nodded to the colorful array. "You don't really think we'll need all those, do you?"

"A man can only hope."

Laughing, Abby opened her arms to him. Only later, much later, did she realize that she'd opened her heart, as well.

The sound of the shower dragged her from a deep, exhausted sleep. She lay facedown, sprawled sideways across a sea of rumpled sheets. Too boneless to do more than lift an eyelid, she tried to determine what time it was.

Shadows lurked in the corners of the loft. Chill air prickled her shoulders and bare backside. It had to be late afternoon, she decided, or early evening.

It took some effort, but she managed to roll over, dragging a handful of the bedspread with her. Cocooned in its warmth, she stared at the massive beams overhead and estimated the time that had passed since she'd yanked on a leather sleeve at the airport yesterday afternoon.

Twenty-six hours, she guessed. Twenty-eight at most.

It seemed longer. Half a lifetime, at least. So much had happened in those hours, not the least of which was the energetic contortions, helpless laughter and soaring, shattering climaxes that had left a scattering of foil packets on the floor beside the bed.

Her thoughts shifted gears, moving from backward to forward. How long had Pete said he'd be in Atlanta? A few days, she thought. Next week, he had to meet that medical board in San Antonio. They had the rest of the holiday weekend before the real world intervened.

Once more she counted. Three days. Another seventy-two hours. A quick smile curved her mouth. The idea of seventy-two more hours with Pete sent joyful anticipation spinning through her limp body.

The very intensity of her joy startled Abby out of her haze of pleasure. Her smile fading, she thought of all the warnings, all the sage advice, she'd ever given Beth. Her words came back to haunt her now.

It wasn't wise to feel so deeply, or so fast.

Rushing into a relationship only opened your heart all the more quickly to the possibility of loss.

Beth hadn't ever heeded her advice, of course. She tumbled into love with all the exuberance of her warm, generous nature, and fell out of it just as quickly. Abby, on the other hand, had never been in love. She realized that now, with cutting clarity. Derek had never generated anything close to the tumultuous pleasure she'd just experienced.

No, not pleasure. With shattering honesty, Abby admitted that she'd found more in Pete's arms than physical pleasure. More than the celebration of life he'd described. It wasn't love...exactly. She couldn't be in love with a man she'd only met yesterday. But this came far too close to that undefinable emotion for her to take lightly.

She was trying to deal with that sobering realization when Pete walked out of the bathroom. His jeans rode low on his hips, and damp sheened his chest. At the sight of the hair curling across his bare skin, Abby's breasts tingled. Swallowing, she pushed the memory of that soft, springy hair abrading her nipples out of her mind. She wasn't quite as successful at dodging the impact of the amusement in his dark eyes, however. That went straight to her heart.

Slinging his towel around his neck, he surveyed her nest of covers. "Are you settled in for the night?"

"I don't know," she answered truthfully.

"Since we're all out of cashews and cocktail olives, I thought you might want to go down to the main lodge for dinner."

When she hesitated, he dipped a knee on the mattress and planted his hands beside her head, caging her in.

"They might have some of that chocolate-rum-raisin cake left," he said temptingly, dropping a kiss on her nose.

Abby grabbed at the excuse. She couldn't think with Pete bending over her like this, let alone sort through the tiny, stinging nuclear reactions his mere proximity set off in her bloodstream.

"That sounds good. Very good!"

She wiggled out from under him, taking the covers with her. Trailing bedspread and sheet, she headed for the bathroom.

"Maybe we can ask the chef to whip up another onion soufflé for us, too."

She closed the door on Pete's comical grimace, then leaned against it. Shutting her eyes, she drew in a deep breath and waited for her heart to stop pinging against her ribs.

Not smart, Abby. Staying here was not smart. She knew that now. She also knew she'd make exactly the same decision, given the same choice.

She had a different choice facing her now, though. One she couldn't put off for seventy-two hours, as much as she wanted to.

Pete was waiting when she came downstairs, a gleam of quiet satisfaction in his eyes.

"I called the hospital while you were dressing. One of the men has already gone home. The other two are being treated for superficial burns, but should be discharged tomorrow."

"Oh, thank goodness!"

He picked up her cloak and settled it on her shoulders. His hands lingered, squeezing gently. "I talked to Orlie. He said to say hello. And thanks."

Abby basked in the glow of their shared triumph during the drive down to the inn. With Pete behind the wheel of the rental car and the tires crunching deep into the gravel, this trip wasn't nearly as nerve-racking as her last attempt to navigate the twisting corkscrew road.

Pete had called ahead for a table, seriously underestimating the pomp and circumstance that simple request would generate. The night manager met them at the front door and ushered them inside. As he escorted them through the lobby, heads turned and guests stopped them to shake hands. Abby's glow quickly gave way to embarrassment. She wasn't used to being the center of attention.

With some relief, she took the seat the manager held out for her at a table set in a paneled alcove. Soft flames flickered in the gas wall fixtures. A candle floated in a cut-crystal rose bowl on the table. The headwaiter beamed at them both and bowed.

"Please, if you'll trust us, the Pines would like to offer you a special menu, prepared in your honor."

Pete deferred to Abby, who nodded.

When the wine steward poured a pale, bubbling aperitif, she fiddled with the stem of her glass, unsure how to broach the subject of what came after dinner. She soon discovered that the presence of a hovering wait staff precluded the kind of conversation she wanted to have with Pete. After dinner, Abby promised herself.

They'd talk after dinner. For now, she'd simply enjoy the incredible array of dishes set before her.

The Pines' chef had prepared a sumptuous feast for the eye, as well as the stomach. Course followed course, each more delicious than the last. Melon soup with lobster and mint. Watercress-and-walnut salad. Turkey breast in shallot-and-brown-butter sauce, served with tomato coulis. And, to Abby's delight, the specialty of the house. The chef himself came to their table to present his golden, puff-crowned masterpiece...along with the thanks of the entire kitchen staff.

After working his way through the feast with the healthy appetite of a good-size man, Pete graciously admitted that the Vidalia onion concoction exceeded even Abby's advance PR work. So much so that he ruefully shook his head at the mention of dessert.

"I don't think I can force any more down tonight. How do scrambled eggs and rum-raisin pancakes for breakfast sound?"

Abby drew in a deep breath and waited to respond until the server had poured a fragrant stream of coffee into their cups and moved away.

"I won't be here for breakfast," she said slowly, forcing herself to meet Pete's eyes. "I'm going home after dinner."

He tilted back in his chair, studying her face in the candlelight. When he didn't respond right away, the small, tight ache in her chest told her she'd made the right decision.

"Regrets already, Abby?"

The soft question stabbed at her heart.

"No! None! But...I think you were right. What happened between us this afternoon was something I've never experienced. That celebration of life you talked about. It was...special, and I want to keep it that way."

Another silence stretched across the table.

"So do I."

Eight

Pete climbed out of the cab and stood on the sidewalk outside the upscale antique and gift shop. The bright Georgia sunshine that had been so noticeably absent the past few days warmed his shoulders. He shifted them under the layer of leather and told himself for the dozenth time that he had no business tracking Abby down at her place of work.

She'd called the shots exactly right the night before last. With brutal honesty, she'd recognized that their afternoon of passion had sprung from an explosive combination of simmering attraction, enforced intimacy and shared danger.

Pete had recognized it, too. He'd always known that the right mix of elements could generate that kind of spontaneous combustion, causing a fire that flared hot and burned fast. Sure enough, it had. When Abby melted into his arms, they'd certainly combusted, then flared so hot that Pete broke out in a sweat whenever he let himself think about those hours with her.

The problem was, the fire inside him hadn't burned out yet.

Against his better judgment, he'd decided to see Abby again before he left for San Antonio tomorrow. Just once more. To see if he could douse this steady, burning need.

Right, O'Brian. Sure.

He knew damn well he didn't want to douse it. He wanted to fan the flame until they were both consumed by it. What he wanted to do and what he would let himself do were two different matters, however. Still, he couldn't leave without seeing her once more. Squaring his shoulders, Pete pushed on the old-fashioned brass latch and walked into another world.

Instantly, a heavy, nose-twitching scent of dried rose petals assaulted him. They were everywhere, in crystal bowls and little trays and baskets scattered across every level surface. Fighting both a grimace and a sneeze, Pete followed the narrow path that led through the crowded shop.

If Things Past specialized in anything in particular, he couldn't decide what it was. His haphazard route took him around arrangements of embroidered pillows, scented candles, dried flowers, ticking grandfather clocks, furniture groupings, and carved sideboards so massive they could have graced the great hall of Stonecross Keep. Framed pictures occupied every inch of wall, and glass-fronted cabinets displayed collections of china, crystal, jewelry and dolls.

Things Past wasn't a man kind of place, he decided. It was too elegant and overscented...much like the woman who glided forward to greet him. Her musky perfume reached Pete long before she did.

"May I help you?"

"I hope so. I'm looking for Abby Davis."

"Abigail? Is she expecting you?"

"No."

The woman's heavily mascaraed eyes drifted down his throat, measured his chest, then returned to his face.

"I'm Marissa DeVries, Abigail's employer. Perhaps if you tell me what you need, I can take care of it for you."

Pete had never felt particularly inclined to discuss his business with strangers. He felt even less inclined to discuss it with a woman who made him want to check his zipper to see if it was all the way up.

"I don't think so." A hint of steel edged into his voice. "Is Abby here?"

Thin, penciled brows arched. "She's in the storeroom. You can go through there."

Pete followed the wave of her hand, dismissing the woman instantly from his mind as the anticipation of seeing Abby crawled all over his skin.

He found her kneeling beside an open crate, surrounded by mounds of air-puffed packing nuggets. Urn-shaped vases, flowered plates and china figurines were lined up in a neat row behind her. Pete paused just outside the door and watched while she lovingly ran a finger tip around the rim of a pink vase. He didn't want to startle her and make her drop the thing. For all he knew, it was a priceless treasure from the court of a Russian czar.

While Abby examined the vase, Pete examined Abby. The sunlight streaming through the back window painted her in shades of blue and gold. She wore a jumpsuit in a deep royal blue that flattered her slender figure and did serious damage to Pete's self-control. Gold filigree buttons decorated the front, and a gold belt emphasized her slim waist. She'd clasped her hair at the back of her neck with an ornamental clip, but, as usual, unruly strands escaped to frame her face.

As enticing as she looked, however, it was the expression in her eyes that tugged at Pete. They glowed with pleasure as she tipped the vase to examine the markings on its bottom. She loved what she did. It was obvious in the careful, loving way she handled the vase, and in the joy it gave her.

He must have made some movement, because she looked up then. Her pleasure yielded to surprise, then to pleasure again. But this was a different kind of pleasure. A polite kind. The kind a woman plastered on her face when a casual acquaintance unexpectedly showed up at her door.

"Pete! What are you doing here?"

He couldn't very well admit he'd been asking himself that exact question since the moment he'd set foot inside the shop.

"I brought you something."

Moving forward, he held out a hand to help her up. She hesitated, then put her fingers in his. He kept his hold loose, but not without effort. Once up, she gave her bottom a quick dusting, then tilted her head.

"Did I forget something at the Pines?"

"No." He dug in his jacket pocket. "I had some time to kill this morning, and came into the city. I was browsing the bookstores, looking for the latest Tom Clancy, when I found this."

Brown paper crackled as she took the package he held out. When she slid the small volume out of the bag and saw its title, she gave a little gasp. Pete decided that small sound of joy more than made up for the long trip downtown.

"Once upon a Mattress," she read aloud, her eyes dancing. *"A History of Bed-Making through the Ages."*

"I flipped through it," Pete offered. "There's a picture and description of a four-poster they say is George IV."

"You're kidding!" She fanned the pages. "Where is it?"

"Page 92. I'm not sure it's your George," he cautioned, angling around to peer over her shoulder as she thumbed the pages.

"Oh, it's not." Disappointment colored her voice, but then she turned and beamed him a smile. "But it's close enough to give me a better idea of its value. Thank you."

It was all he could do not to kiss her. She was standing so close he could see the small golden flecks in her brown eyes and catch her scent, a lighter floral than the overpowering dried roses. Shoving his hands into his pockets to keep from wrapping them around her shoulders, he stepped back.

"You're welcome."

She folded the book against her chest. Tilting her head, she chewed on her lower lip a moment before breaking the small silence that lay between them like a question.

"Would you like to see it? My George, I mean? I took it out of storage yesterday and set it up in the house on Peabody Street."

"Are you moving in already?"

"Not officially, but my offer's been accepted and the Realtor gave me a key." She hugged the book to her chest, smiling happily. "We have to wait for the final appraisal to come back before we close, but the owner didn't mind if I took one piece in."

Pete started to refuse. He'd already stretched his self-discipline about as far as it would stretch. But he couldn't bring himself to squelch Abby's pleasure.

"How could I pass up the chance to see the bed old Mrs. Clement . . ."

"Of the Macon Clements," she interjected, lifting a brow.

He grinned. "...of the Macon Clements...passed to her great-great-granddaughter? Let's go."

As she dug her purse out of the desk drawer and reached for the lightweight wool coat she'd left hanging on a hook behind the door, sensible, responsible Abby couldn't think of anything more foolish than spending another few hours with Pete.

Hadn't she learned her lesson? Hadn't she spent the past two nights working hard not to regret those stolen hours at the Pines? Over and over, she'd told herself that she'd made the right decision when she declined to stay for rum-raisin pancakes. After two sleepless nights, she'd almost convinced herself.

Well, she'd have plenty of nights to work on not regretting her time with Pete. He'd be gone soon, and she'd be up to her ears in the business she'd sunk most of her savings and all of her dreams into. A few more hours was all they'd have.

Abby decided to snatch at them.

First, however, she had to get past the roadblock she knew Marissa would throw in her path. As if on cue, the raven-haired store owner appeared from one of the alcoves. Her thin brows sliced downward when she saw Abby's purse and coat.

"Are you going somewhere?"

"I'm taking an early lunch."

The older woman's glance strayed from her employee to Pete, then back. From the arch look of inquiry in Marissa's face, Abby gathered that she wanted an introduction and an explanation. Having minimized Pete's involvement in her abbreviated account of her unplanned stay at the Pines, Abby wasn't quite up to explaining him to her inquisitive employer now.

"I'll be back in an hour or so," she assured Marissa, dodging the issue.

Clearly annoyed, the shop owner tapped a high-heeled foot on the *faux* marble tiles.

"Really, Abigail, I would appreciate a bit more notice before you juggle the work schedule like this. I have a customer coming in at two for a consultation. I'll need you on the floor then."

Abby headed for the back door, throwing a reassuring smile over her shoulder. "I'll be back."

"Maybe," Pete tossed in.

He shut the door on the shop owner's indignant glare and followed Abby outside.

"Whew! What's the politically correct term for *witch* these days?"

"I wish I knew. Marissa's become . . . a bit more difficult than usual since I gave notice."

She led the way to the rental car furnished by the Pines and unlocked the passenger door for Pete. As she walked around to the driver's side, the bright sunshine put a spring in her step. After the drizzle of the past days, the sky was an impossible blue. The cool, clean

November breeze carried more zip than nip. Abby breathed the crisp air, felt it bubble in her veins.

She paused with her hand halfway to the door handle. As it had at the inn, the intensity of her sensory perceptions startled her. She felt as though she'd suddenly wakened after a heavy sleep.

Sobering, she recognized that this singing in her veins had little to do with the sunshine. Careful, she cautioned herself as she slid behind the wheel. Tread lightly here, Abigail. You have only a few hours.

It took half of one of those hours to reach their destination. Peabody Street wound through a once-fashionable part of Atlanta that had succumbed to age and abandonment and was now fighting its way back. Many of the deteriorating mansions on either side of the wide street still bore the scars of subdivision and graffiti, but a good number had been restored in loving detail with grants from the Georgia Historical Places Preservation Society. The peppering of For Sale and Sold signs planted in the front yards was a sure indication of the resurgence of interest in the area. Abby had staked her future on that renaissance.

Her house stood on a corner, a white two-story Palladian-style home with a columned front porch that was perfect for the wicker furniture and ferns she planned to set out. The entire front facade was skirted by green rhododendrons and azaleas that would blaze with color in the spring. A huge magnolia shaded half the front yard. On the other side, a latticework arch in dire need of a coat of white paint framed a weed-clogged fountain.

Cleaning the fountain would be one of Abby's first priorities. She could almost hear the soft trickle of water from the imp's stone urn as she led Pete up the brick sidewalk. Eagerly she gestured to the three-sided two-story window embrasures on either side of the front door.

"Those bay windows will make perfect display areas. When the shutters are thrown back, you can see right through the house."

Abby fiddled with the touchy lock on the weathered, peeling doors. "I'm going to paint these...."

"I know." His mouth crooked up in the grin that did such funny things to her respiratory system. "Green."

She nodded and pushed the double doors open. She was surprised and pleased that Pete would remember such a small detail.

He did a slow turn in the center of the wide hall that ran from the front to the back of the house, taking in the tall-ceilinged rooms on either side. Abby's gaze followed his, skimming over peeling wallpaper and chunks of plaster missing from the ceiling. She wasn't sure why his opinion mattered so much, but she waited for it anxiously. When he brought his gaze back to hers, it held a touch of doubt.

"You've got your work cut out here."

She chewed on her lower lip. "I know."

"But I can see why you're excited about this place." His doubt folded into a smile. "That crown molding must be eight inches all the way around."

"Ten," Abby said, her breath coming out in a little rush. "It's solid oak, too, not pine. So is the wainscoting in the dining room. Wait until you see it!"

Pete followed her through the downstairs rooms, his initial doubts easing with closer inspection. From what he could see, the basic structure of the house was sound. The fixtures and walls and wiring needed work, though. A lot of work.

Abby didn't minimize the challenge ahead of her. Instead, she seemed to relish it.

"I'm going to do a room at a time," she told him happily. "I'll start with the downstairs, since that will be my main display area, and work my way upstairs. Eventually, I may open some of the upstairs rooms, as well. I'll have to see how it goes, and how much privacy I want to maintain."

Pete followed her up the wide, curving staircase. "You don't anticipate any problems with living and working in the same location?"

"No! I want to showcase my pieces in a home, not cram them into a cluttered, overcrowded rabbit warren like Things Past. My clients will see them as they should be seen, well-used and well-loved."

She stopped outside the room at the front of the upstairs landing, a rueful smile on her face.

"Of course, there is a small problem with that plan. I have a tendency to get too attached to some of my acquisitions . . . like old George here."

Throwing open the double doors to the master suite, she stepped aside. Pete whistled, low and long. The massive four-poster bed stood in solitary splendor in the center of the room. Without mattresses or draperies, it still presented a majestic air, as though it had reclaimed its rightful place in the world.

"So this is Mrs. Clement's legacy."

Strolling into the room, Pete ran a hand over the intricately carved footboard. A pineapple motif was carved into the polished mahogany, matching the knobs that topped the four tall posts.

"How in the world did the movers get it up those stairs?"

"The movers didn't. I did."

"What?"

"It comes apart," Abby told him eagerly. "The posts have several sections that unscrew on wooden dowels. The frame just hooks together. Even the headboard and footboards are made of grooved wooden panels that come apart easily. Furniture used to be crafted that way so it could be transported overland by wagon."

She gripped one of the tall posts and swung in a small arch.

"Yet it's so solid when it's put together. So . . . so enduring."

Pete didn't realize he'd stepped too close until her swing brought her in his direction. Without thinking, he caught her in his arms, surprising himself as much as he did Abby. Her smiling exuberance slipped away, like the sun going behind a cloud. She looked up at him, confusion and wariness creeping into her eyes.

The confusion Pete could understand. He felt it, too. In spades. The wariness made him ache.

He didn't try to deny any longer the need that had brought him into the city this morning to see Abby. He recognized that it wasn't lust, wasn't simply a dangerous mix of chemicals. It went deeper, spread farther through his mind and his heart. If he hadn't seen her face as she showed him her house and her bed, he might have risked asking her to...

To what, O'Brian? Move with him every eighteen or twenty-four months? Keep her treasures in storage and put her dreams on hold for another eight, ten years? Grow more and more bitter with each remote assignment, less tolerant with every short-notice deployment?

Fighting the need to tighten his arms and bring her warmth into his, he tried to make her...and himself...understand.

"I have to leave tomorrow."

"I know."

"I don't want to."

Christ, he hadn't meant to say that! He didn't know why he had, except that it was the truth. Only this particular truth complicated matters far more than he'd intended when he climbed out of that cab.

She swallowed, then managed a shaky smile. "I didn't know that."

That small, trembling curve of her mouth pierced through his shield like a Teflon-coated spear point. He combed his hands through her hair, allowing himself one last touch.

"I could love you, Abby. So easily."

She searched his eyes. Then her smile softened into a gentle acknowledgment that tore at his soul.

"You did love me," she replied. "So wonderfully."

"I can't stop thinking about those hours we spent together."

"I've thought about them once or twice myself."

Pete forced himself to go on. He didn't want any shadows or unanswered questions between them when he left.

"Sweetheart, if I could, and if you'd let me, I'd curl up with you in that bed and spend the rest of my life there."

Her lips parted, closed, then parted again, as if the words she wanted wouldn't come.

"But you can't," she got out at last.

"No."

"And I wouldn't let you. I've seen you in action, remember? I know how good you are. Despite that twisted piece of metal you carry around like a hair shirt—or maybe because of it—I suspect you're one of the best."

She tried for light and easy, but Pete saw the hurt in her eyes. Dammit! He'd sworn he'd never cause another woman that kind of hurt.

"I won't ask you to put aside all your dreams and come with me, and I can't ask you to wait for me. Aside from the fact that I don't have the right, it wouldn't be fair to you."

"Maybe..." She wet her lips. "Maybe I'm a better judge of what's fair for me."

"I've been down this road once, Abby. I've seen what happens when there are too many goodbyes between a man and a woman. I don't want that to happen to us."

Abby pulled out of his arms and turned away, refusing to let him see the piercing ache his words gave her. And the anger. She'd discovered that she didn't like being compared to Pete's former wife. Any more than she liked his assumptions about what would and wouldn't be fair to her.

Shoving her hurt into a small corner of her heart to be examined later, she drew her dignity around her. As with Derek, she wouldn't try to bind a man who wasn't sure he wanted her.

"Look, I appreciate your concern over what would or wouldn't be fair for me, but I'm a big girl. I make my own decisions. I have for a long time. That's why I chose to leave the inn when I did, before we both—" she gave a helpless shrug "—before we started worrying about goodbyes."

Pete raked a hand through his hair. Abby saw frustration in the abrupt gesture and in the wire-tight lines of his body. She might have sympathized with him, but she was feeling more than a little wired herself right now. There was no point in prolonging the agony, for either of them.

"I'd better get back to the shop."

He studied her face for long moments, then nodded. "Yeah, I guess you'd better."

Abby left the bedroom first. Trailing a hand along the smooth, well-worn banister, she started down the stairs. From the corner of her eye, she saw Pete give the bed a last long look, then firmly shut the bedroom doors.

They made the drive back downtown in uneasy silence. They really didn't have anything more to say to each other, Abby realized as she negotiated the traffic. They'd said it all. All that could be said between them, anyway. Except those damnable goodbyes.

They made them quickly—Abby first, then Pete.

She hoped that his medical board went well.

He wished her success with her new home.

Then they shared a brief kiss that satisfied neither of them.

Abby stood beside the rental car while he slipped on a pair of aviator sunglasses, shoved his hands in his jacket pockets and turned to leave.

She made it to the back door of the shop before she swung around, her hand on the brass knob and her heart in her throat.

"Pete?"

He turned, his eyes shielded behind the mirrored lenses. "Yes?"

"Just for the record, I could love you, too. Easily."

Nine

The white-coated surgeon dropped a thick manila folder on his desk and swiveled to face his patient. "It's the classic good-news-bad-news scenario, Sergeant O'Brian. Which do you want first?"

Pete tugged on his uniform coat to square it over his shoulders. After five days of tests and more tests at Wilford Hall, the huge medical complex located on Lackland Air Force Base, just south of San Antonio, he was ready for the final verdict.

"Give it to me the way that makes most sense, Doc."

The surgeon drummed his fingers on the sheaf of X rays and lab reports, marshaling his thoughts. A lieutenant colonel with two rows of framed degrees behind his desk and a blunt, no-nonsense air of authority, Dr.

McMillin took his job seriously. So seriously he'd requested that Pete meet him in his office on Saturday morning, instead of waiting for his scheduled appointment on Monday.

"Your right anterior cruciate ligament is shot to hell. Your last jump shredded what little was left of it after twenty-plus years of hitting the ground harder than a body is supposed to."

Pete's mouth curved. "Is that the bad news or the good news?"

"The bad. And it gets worse." The surgeon's gray eyes met Pete's steadily. "Our initial tests indicated there might be enough ligament tissue left for us to weave in a synthetic fiber and restructure the ACL, but it appears there isn't."

Although the second series of tests he'd gone through had given Pete the suspicion that the damage was more extensive than he'd thought, the verdict hit him square in the chest. With more than twenty-two years in the jump business, he accepted bad knees and spinal compression as a risk of his profession. But there were bad knees, and then there were bad knees. Most could be repaired enough for a man to return to jump status. From what the colonel was saying, it seemed his couldn't.

He leveled the doc a straight look. "I hope you're not going to suggest that the good news is a total knee replacement?"

They both knew that an artificial knee would take him off jump status permanently.

"No, I know that's the last option you'd consider," Colonel McMillin replied, passing a hand over his buzz-cut gray hair. "What I want to talk to you about is a new procedure we're testing. It involves fitting a plastic cap over your own bone. We attach the muscle to that with artificial ligaments."

"I've heard of the procedure," Pete replied. "I've also heard it hasn't been all that successful to date."

"It's had mixed results," McMillin admitted. "A civilian surgeon who specializes in sports-related injuries reports some success. We've tried it twice here, once on a teenager who took a body block during football practice and once on another PJ."

Pete knew the man the doc was referring to, a shoe-leather-tough Vietnam vet, a good troop and a damn fine PJ. He now served behind a desk.

"Let me be sure I've got it straight, Doc." He leaned forward, wanting his options laid clear. "If this plastic cap works, I go back on jump status. If it doesn't, I don't."

"It's not quite that cut-and-dried, O'Brian. This is still an experimental procedure. We haven't had a good take with it yet. If it works, then we'll evaluate whether you should start hitting the chutes again."

Pete nodded, his eyes hooded. "Fair enough."

"Think about it over the weekend. If you decide you want to be our third guinea pig, call my secretary Monday morning and we'll set you up for surgery."

Pete walked out of the multistory medical center, his highly glossed jump boots sounding a steady beat on the concrete sidewalk. Bright Texas sunlight glinted on the silver *US*s pinned to his lapels and on the shiny wings positioned above the rows of ribbons on his chest. With the unconscious arrogance that came with being a PJ, he squared his maroon beret on his head, then tugged it to precisely the right angle over his brow.

As he made his way toward his rental car, a distant drumbeat carried on the morning air. He stopped, cocking his head as the sound took on a familiar rhythm. He hadn't marched to that beat in years, but he identified it immediately. The basic trainees were marching onto the parade field adjacent to the hospital complex in preparation for their graduation ceremony.

As the center for all air force basic military training, Lackland conducted a formal parade every six weeks or so to mark the recruits' graduation from boot camp. Since the base was also the site of the ten-week PJ in-doctrination course that followed immediately after basic training, Pete had attended a good number of these parades prior to interviewing the candidates for the PJ career field. He always enjoyed the ceremony. The color and pageantry of the event stirred something deep within him.

The beat of that distant drum now drew him like a siren's call. After his session with the doc this morning and too many long nights of thinking about Abby, he needed to focus on something outside himself. Something simple. Something basic.

Something he could enjoy, then walk away from without a sense of having left a part of himself behind.

Dropping his car keys into his pocket, he headed for the broad, grassy field a half mile or so away. He stood down field, well away from the bleachers filled with proud parents and spouses, excited children, invited guests and the uniformed training instructors who'd worked twenty hours a day for the past six weeks to turn raw recruits into disciplined airmen.

The troops were massed across the field from the bleachers and the reviewing stand, with the colors in the center. The Stars and Stripes waved in the breeze. Several foreign flags ranged next to it, in recognition of the students from other nations sent to Lackland for basic training. Behind them flew the service flags, heavy with battle streamers earned during bloody engagements on land, on sea and in hostile skies.

Pete's eyes fixed on the blue air force flag. Even from this distance, he could pick out several of the distinctive streamers. They matched the campaign ribbons he wore on his chest. He'd served in his share of distant battles, and flown through a few hostile skies.

Pulling his gaze from the flags, he let it drift down squadron after squadron of short-sheared, blue-suited troops standing at parade rest, legs spread, hands clasped loosely behind their backs.

Christ, they looked so young! And so damned eager. He felt a tug of envy for the future that stretched so limitlessly before them. What honor would they bring to the just-issued uniforms they wore so proudly? How many battle streamers would they add to the flags waving in the breeze? How many of them would end their careers too soon, like Carrington?

Pete slipped his hand into his pants pocket, searching through the keys and pocket change for a twisted scrap of metal. His eyes on the field, he fingered the constant reminder of his heavy responsibilities to those young, eager rookies.

He shoved those responsibilities to the back of his mind when an officer quickstepped to the center of the field and faced the massed squadrons.

"Soooooound adjutant's call!"

The military band belted out a few short chords, alerting the troops and the visitors to the start of the ceremonies.

"Bring your groups to at-tennnn-shun!"

One after another, group and squadron commanders echoed the adjutant's bellowed order. The air reverberated with the bellowed commands. Five hundred chins lifted. A thousand heels clicked. Shoulders squared. Chests puffed. Guidons whipped up, and blue-and-gold squadron pennants snapped in the breeze.

Unconsciously Pete pulled back his shoulders and dropped his hands in loose fists at his side. His pulse accelerating in a quick, steady beat, he listened to the ritual announcements that signaled the start of the ceremonies.

When the reviewing party arrived and the colors marched forward, Pete came to rigid, square-shouldered attention. At the first note of the national anthem, his right arm sliced up in sync with all the others on the field. Palm blade-straight, fingertips just touching his brow, he stood tall. The emotions that comrades-in-arms rarely, if ever, admitted to pounded through his veins . . . the same emotions that drove men and women to leave their homes and their families and don a uniform that made them targets for hostile forces.

Pride. Patriotism. A sense of belonging to a larger community. A need to return some measure of service to the nation that nourished them.

Throughout the ceremonies, he stood at the end of the field. He barely heard the introduction of the reviewing party. Watched with abstracted interest when the officers massed at the center and marched forward, then returned to lead their troops. Listened with only a part of himself to the stirring remarks by the commanding general. His thoughts stayed focused entirely on the troops.

The future belonged to them. To these men and women who stepped out in massed squadrons, then columned right and hit their stride to the stirring beat of the air force anthem. Arms whipping up, they saluted the reviewing officer as they marched past. From where he stood, alone and proud, Senior Master Sergeant O'Brian saluted them.

As they passed, one squadron after another, Pete remembered how he'd stepped out some twenty-two years ago. Like these eager men and women, he'd marched off this field, straight into two decades of excitement and routine, incredible challenges and occasional frustrations. He'd made decisions during those two decades that he regretted, certainly. There had been moments he'd sell his soul to relive. But for twenty-two years, he'd given everything in him he had to give.

Now he might have a chance to march another few years into that future.

Or into a different future.

I could love you, too. Easily.

The words echoed faintly over the tromp of marching feet. They wove through the chords of stirring, martial music.

He could see Abby standing with one hand on the door to the shop. The sunlight had made a fuzzy halo of her hair and dusted her skin. Lord, she had the most beautiful skin. Pete's fists bunched tighter.

Of all the goodbyes he'd ever said, that one had hurt the most. It still hurt. This time, though, he suspected that neither time nor distance would ease the ache.

I could love you, too.

Pete waited until after the last squadron had passed in review. He stood silent while the airmen tossed their caps in the air in exuberant glee. Then he walked back to the hospital parking lot, searched out his rental car and drove to the visiting senior NCO quarters.

Tossing the car keys and his maroon beret on the coffee table, he unbuttoned his blue coat and loosened his tie. Hands shoved into his pockets, he stood at the window. He had some hard thinking to do before he reached for the phone sitting on the desk.

When the phone shrilled, Abby was literally up to her ears in boxes.

She'd decided to take advantage of her Saturday afternoon off to start packing her personal things. The professionals would move the large pieces, but she wanted to sort through and wrap the smaller items herself. Given her penchant for collecting treasures, it was a laborious task. Thank goodness Beth had called from L.A. and promised to come over and help when her flight landed in Atlanta later this afternoon. Her sister always needed time for her internal clock to reset itself after an international run. Packing would be as good a way as any to work off her body's confusion over abrupt time zone changes, she'd insisted.

Abby lifted a stack of books from the bookshelf and tucked them into a box, mulling over the brief call. Beth had asked how her fiancé had taken her nonappearance at the wedding, of course. The news of Jordy's unexpected deployment to the world's current hot spot had shocked Beth into a long, tense silence. She'd hung up shortly afterward, but not before she told Abby that she needed her sage advice and counsel when she got into Atlanta.

Sighing, Abby reached for another stack of books. She didn't feel up to dishing out advice to Beth, or to anyone else, for that matter. In fact, she heartily wished there was someone she could turn to for a little counseling herself. She hadn't felt this...this empty in years.

She should be simmering with excitement right now. She should be tucking her things into boxes with the joyous expectation of unpacking them in the old, well-loved home she'd always longed for. The house on Peabody Street was all but hers.

True, the appraisal had returned with an estimated value some four thousand dollars lower than expected. Her Realtor had gone back to renegotiate the price with the owners, but Abby had already privately decided to eat the difference if they proved recalcitrant, since she'd budgeted for the original amount anyway.

So where was the thrill of excitement that usually rippled through her when she thought about her house? What had happened to the pleasure she felt each time she stopped by the place after work and wandered through its rooms? Why didn't her heart jump at the thought of sleeping in her four-poster bed?

There was only one answer to all the questions that now plagued her, and he hadn't called. Not once since he'd left Atlanta.

Damn O'Brian, anyway. How could he have walked into her life, cut a swath through her dreams and walked out again, just like that?

Even more to the point, how could she have let him?

Abby sat back on her heels, the books clutched in her hands. He was probably on his way back to England by now. To the air base located close to... Where was it? Stonecross Keep. Vague descriptions of square stone towers, black-beamed ceilings and trestle tables drifted through her mind, followed by an image of Pete sprawled in the love seat opposite hers, his long legs stretched toward the fire as he'd dug through his memory for the details she demanded.

Almost immediately, another image crowded that one aside. Of her and Pete sharing the same love seat. Of his hands massaging her frigid toes with a gentleness that made her ache almost as much as the memory of their passionate hours in the loft.

The shrill of the phone ripped through her fragile memories and laid her wide open for a rush of hope. Dumping the books in a heap on the floor, she shoved aside a stack of boxes and snatched up the receiver.

"Hello."

"Abby?"

The sound of a woman's husky voice sent disappointment lancing into her heart. It was all she could do to force out a reply.

"Yes?"

"It's me, Cherry."

Abby summoned a smile and a warm greeting. As soon as the polite preliminaries were over, Cherry plunged right into the reason for her call.

"Listen, sweetie, I have a big favor to ask you. I know it's an imposition, but you're the only other woman I know in Atlanta, and even if you weren't, I feel like we're friends. Please say you'll do it."

Abby smiled at the breathless, excited rush. "Sure, if I can."

"Would you be my maid of honor? Tonight? At the Pines?"

"What?"

"Irv pushed his divorce through as soon as we got back to Dallas," Cherry reported, happiness bubbling like a fountain in her voice. "He signed the papers last night, and we flew back to Atlanta this morning to get the blood test and the license. Georgia's still his legal residence for tax purposes, you know."

"Er, no, I didn't know."

"It is, and we are. Getting married tonight, I mean! Can you believe it it?"

Abby grinned. "I believe it! Just out of curiosity, though, what happened to the Lincoln?"

Cherry's infectious gurgle of laughter came over the line. "Irv gave it to his ex . . . after I reminded him that we'd pretty well worn out the shocks, anyway."

"Good for both of you!"

Cherry sobered. "Irv says he realized something up there on that ridge, when he was working on Orlie with you. Life's too uncertain to take anything for granted. He says sometimes you just gotta go for it. You know, take that leap . . . like you're doing, sinking all your savings into your new shop."

Before Abby could respond to that, she rushed on. "So he called the mayor. Remember her? The one who tried to marry you and Irv?"

"I remember."

"She's going to perform the ceremony, and Orlie's going to give me away, and I'd really love it if you'd be my maid of honor."

"I . . ."

"I know this is awfully short notice. I would have called you earlier, but we weren't sure we could get the blood tests and the license done, and then we were rushing around so much I didn't have time to call. But say you'll do it!"

"Of course I will. I'd be honored."

"Oh, Abby, thank you! We'll send a car for you. Is an hour from now okay? The ceremony's at six."

"You don't need to send a car. I got my van back yesterday, in better condition than when I bought it. I'll drive up."

"No, you won't. We're doing this right. Tell me your address and we'll send a limo. Oh, and Abby?"

"Yes?"

"You'd better wear something white, for tradition's sake, because I'm wearing red!"

"Now why doesn't that surprise me?"

Laughing, Abby hung up. Cherry's contagious happiness kept her smiling as she weaved her way through her scattered possessions. She'd have to shuck her jeans and grubby t-shirt and grab a quick shower if she was going to be ready by the time the limo arrived.

She walked into the bedroom thinking how strange it was that she'd never been to the Pines before, and now she'd been asked to participate in her second wedding there in less than a week. Hopefully, this wedding would come off better than the last one. With any luck, Cherry and Irv wouldn't have to bundle under layers and layers of blankets to keep warm when they shared that sybaritic bed in the honeymoon cottage.

At the memory of the hours she'd spent with Pete in that huge bed, she froze with her jeans peeled halfway down her hips. Breath suspended, she waited for the ache to pass.

It didn't. It pooled in a spot just under her heart and stayed there, a heavy, constant hurt.

Shoving her jeans off, Abby shook her head. Sweet heavens, how could she have been such a fool? After all those years of giving Beth advice, of trying to keep her from tumbling in and out of love, she'd done exactly the same thing. Or almost the same thing. She'd tumbled into love, apparently, but she hadn't quite reached the "out of it" stage yet. She was beginning to suspect she never would.

Unlike Beth, though, she hadn't had the courage to reach out and grab at that love. Steady, cautious Abby had retreated into her safe world and watched Pete walk away, just as she'd watched Derek What's-his-name walk out of her arms into her sister's charmed circle.

She hadn't even tried to hold on to Pete, she thought in disgust. Or find the middle ground between her dreams and his duty. She'd let him go back to his life, and she'd stayed in hers. So here she was, surrounded by cardboard boxes and about to act as maid of honor at another woman's wedding.

Some life, Abigail. Some dreams!

She sank down on the edge of the bed, her mind churning. Gradually her hurt became anger at herself, then slowly tipped into something else. Something less painful. More positive. Determination gathered, bit by bit, at the outer corners of her heart. Then it folded in on itself, until it became an insistent, demanding force.

Dammit, Irv was right. More or less. Sometimes a person just had to go for it—only in this case, Abby had gone for the wrong thing. For a supposedly intelligent woman, she'd taken far too long to realize that a home was so much more than just a house. It was shared laughter, and sour-cream potato chips before the fire, and someone warming your toes for you on a cold night.

That kind of home you could make anywhere, she told herself fiercely. It didn't have to be on Peabody Street, or even in Atlanta.

Pete's highly mobile career didn't have to mean only goodbyes. So he spent a lot of time in the air! He had to come down sometime, didn't he? And when he did, she'd be there. She'd welcome him home, just as Mrs. Clement's descendants had welcomed their men for generation after generation. She'd take her heart and her hopes and her portable George IV wherever Pete went.

Her determination flowered into a fierce, pounding joy, tempered by just a touch of reality.

Okay, so he hadn't said he wanted her with him wherever he went. He hadn't even said that he loved her, exactly. Only that he *could* love her. Well, any woman worth her salt ought to be able to turn that *could* into *does*.

And if she didn't? The voice of caution that she could never quite shake struggled to be heard over the pounding of her heart. If she failed to convince Pete? What then?

Then she'd pick up the pieces and go on. But at least she would have tried. For once in her life, she would have thrown aside all caution and common sense and followed her heart, not her head.

She sat absolutely still on the bed for several long moments, then reached out and yanked the phone off the nightstand. Her hands trembling, she started dialing.

Ten

Pete strode out of Atlanta's airport with more adrenaline coursing through his veins than he'd pumped before his very first jump.

He hadn't taken time to change out of his uniform. After placing a quick call to the hospital and another to his overseas unit, he'd barely taken time to throw his things in his carryall before checking out of the visiting NCO quarters. He'd arrived at the San Antonio airport just as a flight to Atlanta was boarding. It had taken some fast ticketing and a first-class seat, but he'd made the flight.

Moments after the plane touched down at its destination, he was out the door and heading for the airport exit. This time, no flushed, curly-haired creature in a black cloak tugged at his sleeve to stop him. This time, he couldn't shift his carryall into his left hand and sweep her against him with his right, as he ached to do. But he would. Dammit, he would. Before he boarded the plane that would take him back to England, he was going to hold her and kiss her and try to convince her that they'd already said all their goodbyes.

He probably should call ahead, he thought as he hailed a cab. Abby might not want to see him. Hell, she might not even want to talk to him after their last session, but what he had to say couldn't be said over the phone.

Slinging his bag and himself into the cab, he gave the driver directions to Things Past. The trip into the city seemed to take twice as long as it had the last time. Curbing his simmering impatience with some effort, he used the time to marshal his arguments.

When they pulled up at the shop, Pete was half out of the cab before he saw the Closed sign on the door. His colorful curse raised the cabbie's brows.

"Got a problem, Sarge?"

"Yeah, I do."

Pete eyed the sign in disgust. He hadn't counted on the shop closing early on Saturday afternoons. He had no idea where Abby lived. Where she *planned* to live, yes. But where she currently resided, no. He climbed back into the cab and slammed the door.

"Pull over at the next phone booth you see. I have to check an address."

With the taxi idling behind him, he flipped through the fat phone directory. As he'd expected, he found no listing for Abigail Davis. When he saw the multiple A. Davises in the directory, he muttered another curse and pulled out the piece of paper Jordy had given him containing both Beth's and Abby's phone numbers. The paper unfolded easily along well-worn crease lines. He'd taken it out more times than he could count this past week and stared at the number scrawled across it.

Eyes narrowed, he checked the scribbled phone numbers against those listed in the directory. Moments later, he climbed back in the cab and slammed the door.

"Ten-sixteen Philmont, and hurry."

The cabbie grinned. "Fasten your seat belt. This baby moves about as fast as the F-4s I used to work on."

Reining in his impatience, Pete met his gaze in the mirror. "How long were you in?"

"Only one hitch. Vietnam was enough for me. Though I hafta tell you, I never took the flak at Tan Son Nhut that I take when I drive through some parts of this city."

Pete listened with half an ear to the vet's rambling and occasionally raunchy stories of his days in the service. With each turn of the tires, he felt his control slipping closer and closer to the edge of its restraint.

When they pulled up in front of a mellow brick-fronted apartment complex, the sight of Abby's brown van kicked his pulse into overdrive. His heart slamming against his ribs, Pete paid off the cabbie, wished him luck, then leaned on the doorbell of 1016.

He'd anticipated surprise.

He'd hoped for at least a cool welcome.

What he hadn't counted on was that the woman who opened the door would take one astonished look at him, turn deathly pale and crumple in a faint.

"Christ!"

Pete caught her before she hit the tiled floor of the foyer. Scooping her into his arms, he kicked the door shut and carried her into an apartment that in ordinary circumstances might have been spacious and airy. Right now, it looked as though a Scud missile had zeroed in on it.

Boxes were scattered everywhere, some empty, some sealed, others half packed. Pete couldn't find a chair or sofa that didn't have books or linens or knick-knacks stacked on it. He stood in the middle of the room, his burden a dead weight in his arms, and tried to find someplace to lay her. Finally he lifted a boot and nudged a stack of linens off a plush Victorian armchair.

She gave a little groan when he eased her into the chair. Pete stared down at her for a moment, then carved a path into the kitchen and rummaged through more boxes until he found a saucepan. Deciding it would have to do, he half filled it with water and returned to the living room.

"Beth! Beth, wake up!"

He loosened the dark blue tie of her airline uniform, slid a hand under her neck to raise her head and held the pot to her lips.

"Here, take some water."

When the liquid trickled into her mouth, Beth sputtered and choked and came awake. Before Pete could remove the pot, she lunged up and knocked it aside. Cold water hit him squarely in the face. He jerked back, only to have Beth grab his lapels and follow him.

"It's Jordy, isn't it? Oh, God, I know it's Jordy."

"No..."

"Tell me!" She clung to him like a burr, sobbing. "Tell me, Pete! Is he dead?"

He closed his hands over hers, trying to ease her frantic grip. "No, he's not dead!"

She moaned. "He's wounded. Isn't he? He's wounded and calling for me." Tears poured down her cheeks. "It's all my fault. If I hadn't run out on him..."

"Beth..."

"Where is he, Pete? Tell me. I'll go to him. I can—"

"Beth, calm down! Jordy's not injured. Or he wasn't when I called back to the unit a few hours ago."

His words finally penetrated her hiccuping sobs.

"He's okay? Really?"

Pete's voice gentled. "Really."

She sagged against him in relief.

Pete patted her awkwardly on the back, waiting for her sobs to cease. His patience ran out before her sniffles.

Easing her away, he looked down into the face that he, like Jordy, had once thought perfect. Her features were finer than her sister's, and her hair was a paler, silkier blond. But she didn't have Abby's firm chin or her wide, full mouth. Nor, Pete remembered belatedly, did she have her incisive intelligence.

"Why are you wearing all your ribbons and stuff?" she asked through watery sniffs. At his blank look, she waved a hand distractedly. "That's...that's what frightened me so much."

Pete couldn't help himself. He had to ask. "My ribbons scared you?"

"I thought—" She gulped. "You know, like in the movies. Men in full dress uniform show up at the front door to...to notify the next of kin."

Pete was forced to point out the obvious. "Beth, you're not Jordy's next of kin."

It was a mistake. Her eyes teared up again.

"I know. But I want to be. I think."

Pete let that one pass. He had more important things on his mind than Beth's mercurial relationship with her almost-groom. Tugging her hands free of his lapels, he did a quick scan of the cluttered room.

"Where's Abby?"

"Abby?"

"Your sister?"

She sniffed. "Why do you want to see Abby?"

"I need to talk to her about a personal matter. Where is she?"

Her tears drying, she looked up at Pete in surprise. "A personal matter? With Abby?"

"Beth..."

The low, strangled snarl sent her back a pace. "She's...she's at the Pines."

"The Pines?"

"She went to a wedding. Another wedding."

Her chin wobbled for a moment, and Pete braced himself for more tears. Bravely Beth fought them back.

"She left the strangest note. It's in the kitchen. Evidently her dentist is getting married to a woman named...Peaches, I think it was."

It took Pete only a second or two to connect the dentist with Irv, and Irv with Peaches, a.k.a. Cherry. Evidently the periodontist had finally decided to claim his woman. Good for him!

Beth's flawless face clouded with confusion. "I don't know why Abby didn't mention going to this wedding when I called her earlier."

Pete didn't know, either, and didn't particularly care. He didn't intend to wait any longer to stake his own claim.

"Did you drive here?" he asked Beth.

"No, I took a cab from the airport."

"Do you know where Abby keeps the keys to the van?"

His curt question triggered another confused frown.

"That's something else I don't understand. The Antiquemobile got a complete face-lift while I was gone, and Abby never said a word about it. Although I suppose she had to get it in good working order before she goes on this trip."

"What trip?"

"Her note said she was going on a trip tomorrow. To Stone Keep." Beth's brow knit. "Maybe she meant Stone Mountain. That's only a few miles from here, though why she'd have the van—"

She gave a startled squeak as Pete gripped her arms.

"Stonecross Keep? Did Abby say she was going to Stonecross Keep?"

"That . . . that might have been it. I'll have to check the note."

Pete felt as though a flare had just been set off inside him. A burst of white-hot fire spiraled through his chest, then burned with a searing heat. He stood rock-still for several moments, waiting for the flame to subside. Seconds later, he realized this was one conflagration that wasn't going to burn itself out.

The fact that Abby had decided to go to England told him that she might be feeling the same steady flame.

While Pete tried to steady his rocketing emotions, Beth worried her lower lip with perfect white teeth and put her own interpretation on her sister's cryptic note.

"It isn't like Abby to just take off like this. I hope she's not sick or something."

"She's something," Pete said under his breath. "I sure hope she's something."

Abby tried not to grin as she matched her step to the recorded sounds of the wedding march and glided down the aisle formed by rows of chairs. Despite her best efforts, the astounded expressions on the faces of the handful of guests who'd hastily assembled for the wedding had her mouth curving. Quickly she buried her nose in her lavish bouquet to hide her laughter.

With her face bathed in the heady scent of long-stemmed red roses, she traveled the length of the banquet room toward the small party waiting in front of the massive stone fireplace. Cherry followed, on Orlie Taggert's arm. If Irv saw anything amiss in his bride's attire, Abby couldn't tell it from his beaming face.

Mayor Calvin, on the other hand, gaped when she caught her first sight of the bridal party.

True to her word, Cherry had chosen to wear red. Bright, traffic-light red. Eye-popping red, accented with thousands of sequins. They shimmered on the bride's formfitting dress and shaped her magnificent bosom. More sequins dotted the short veil pinned to her upswept flaming red hair. Even the streamers trailing from her huge bouquet of crimson roses glittered with spangles. The only nonred article on her person was the antique sterling-silver pin studded with blue topaz that she'd borrowed from Abby.

Abby herself was dressed more like a bride than the bride. Following Cherry's instructions, she'd worn off-white, an ankle-length skirt in a creamy ivory wool and a matching hand-knit tunic studded with tiny drop pearls. Thank goodness she had. Any other color would have clashed horribly with the Cherry's dazzling fire-engine-red dress.

Still fighting a grin, she nodded to Irv and the mayor, then stepped to the side. The bride placed a kiss on Orlie's leathery cheek, released his arm, then moved into position. Cherry stood a good six inches taller than her groom, and anyone who saw the look they exchanged at that moment knew height didn't make a whisker of difference to either one of them. Gripping hands, they faced each other.

The mayor cleared her throat. Her weathered face creasing, she looked from Cherry to Abby. Then she winked at Irv.

"You sure you've got the right bride this time?"

He grinned. "I'm sure."

"Well, let's get you two—"

She broke off as the doors at the back of the banquet room rattled. Irv threw a look over his shoulder, then gave Cherry a quick grin.

"Hey, my office manager must have finally tracked Pete down. He made it!"

Abby swung around, her nails digging into the stems of her rose bouquet. Disbelieving, she watched a tall, broad-shouldered figure stand aside while Beth rushed into the banquet room. For probably the first time in her adult life, Abby didn't spare a thought for her sister. She barely gave her a glance. Her entire being was focused on the man who followed Beth in.

Seeing him in uniform for the first time, Abby knew that the agonizing decision she'd made an hour ago was the right one. He wore his uniform easily, but she saw the pride that went into its tailored fit, the boots polished to a mirror gloss, and the precise alignment of his silver wings above his ribbons. He belonged in air force blue.

And she belonged with him.

He closed the doors behind him and leaned against them, his mouth curving in the crooked grin that made Abby's lungs forget to pump. Across the length of the banquet room, their eyes locked.

At that moment, her last doubts vanished. Wherever they went, they'd go together. Whatever bed they slept in, they'd sleep together. Tears prickled her lids, and she had to bury her nose in her bouquet once more to keep from crying during Cherry's and Irv's exchange of vows.

Any hope she might have harbored that she'd get Pete alone after the brief ceremony vanished as soon as a laughing, radiant Cherry released Irv from a passionate embrace. Hooking one arm through Irv's, she used the other to signal to Pete to join the small group milling around the wedding party.

When he approached, Irv thumped him on the back in a hearty greeting. "I'm glad you got my message. Thanks for coming, buddy."

"I didn't get your message, but you're welcome." Smiling, Pete bent and gave Cherry a kiss on one cheek. "You make a stunning bride."

She laughed up at him. "I do, don't I?"

Over Irv's shining bald crown, Pete caught Abby's smile. She looked so vibrant, so joyous, so... welcoming, that everything he'd planned to say to her got lost in the need to hold her.

He'd taken exactly half a step toward her when the mayor's sturdy form planted itself in front of him.

"Nice to see you in these parts again, O'Brian." She shook his hand, her shrewd gaze assessing his rows of ribbons. "I suppose it's too much to hope that you're thinking 'bout staying. I wasn't just pushing air around when I said we could use a man like you."

Pete flashed Abby another look.

"As a matter of fact," he said slowly, "I have been thinking about staying. Permanently."

Abby's eyes rounded in surprise. Edging around the mayor and Irv, Pete moved swiftly to her side.

"I didn't plan to tell you like this."

She swallowed. "Tell me what?"

Before he could answer, Beth wedged her way through the crowd and joined them.

"Abby, are you all right?"

"I'm fine. Tell me what, Pete?"

"Are you sure?" The younger woman peered into her sister's face anxiously. "You look a little pale."

Abby ignored her sister. "Tell me what, Pete?"

He glanced at the faces surrounding them. Their avid interest told Pete his chances of getting Abby alone right now were nonexistent. Resigning himself to saying what he had to say before the curious audience, he reached for her hand.

"I've put in my papers, sweetheart. I called my commander this morning to let him know. I'm getting out of the service as soon as I get back to England and process the retirement."

Dismay flooded her brown eyes. "Oh, Pete, why?"

His stomach lurched at her stricken expression. Dismay wasn't quite the reaction he'd been hoping for.

"Because I gave the air force my future once," he said quietly, his fingers gripping hers. "It was all I wanted then, all I thought I needed. Now I know I need more. I need you."

"But you didn't have to give it up. I—"

He cut her off, his hold on her hand tight and hard.

"I don't want any more goodbyes between us, Abby. I want to stay with you always. I want to curl up with you in Mrs. Clement's bed, and help you turn the house on Peabody Street into a home."

Her dismay gave way to an almost comical chagrin. Pete didn't care for that reaction much more than he had the last.

"If you'll let me, Abby, I want to share your dreams."

His gut twisting, he waited for her reply. To his profound relief, her mouth lifted in a tremulous smile.

"You can curl up with me anywhere. For as long as you want."

He loosened his death grip on her hand and reached for her.

"But..."

The small caveat froze him in place. "But?"

"But I think you should know, I withdrew my offer on the house on Peabody Street."

"What?"

His exclamation got lost in Beth's startled gasp.

"Abby! You gave up your house?"

The stunned expressions on the faces of the two people she loved most in the world made Abby take a deep breath. She'd sort out Beth's feelings later. Right now, all that mattered to her was Pete's.

"The appraisal came in too low, which gave me a legal out. So I called the Realtor and told her I didn't want the house." Her tentative smile widened, then spilled into a grin. "I also mentioned that I was leaving for an extended stay in England."

"England!" Beth squeaked.

Cherry gave a low, throaty chuckle and gripped Irv's arm with red-polished nails. "Good for you, sweetie! Go for it!"

Even Mayor Calvin got into the act. Her face folding into crags and valleys, she glanced from Abby to Pete.

"Well, well . . . Looks like we've got another bride, and the right groom, this time."

Abby ignored them all. Her whole being was centered on the man standing before her.

Her heart gave a painful thump of joy as Pete's blue eyes lit with laughter. . . and with a love that warmed her all the way to her toes.

"So you gave up your house, and I gave up the air force." He opened his arms to her. "I sure glad we've still got George III."

"George IV."

With a strangled sound that hovered somewhere between a sob and a laugh, she fell into his welcoming arms. His mouth was warm and hard and demanding. Hers asked for more, much more.

When he scooped her up in his arms, her stomach tightened in joyous anticipation. Whatever she asked for, he would give her.

"We'll call you as soon as we get the license and the blood tests," Pete told the grinning mayor. "It may be a few days."

"Anytime, O'Brian."

They were halfway to the back of the banquet room when Abby realized she was still clutching her bouquet.

"Pete! Wait a moment!"

Twisting in his arms, she tossed the roses in a long arc. Beth caught them, her face a study in confusion and doubtful happiness for her sister.

"Hold these for me, Sissy. And call Gulliver's Travels, would you? Tell them I need to change my reservation to London. I want to go on flight...?" She arched an inquiry at Pete.

"You don't have to go all that way with me," he told her softly. "I'll be back within a few weeks. I promise."

She wrapped her arms around his neck. "Oh, no, my darling. No more goodbyes, remember? Whither thou goest, I'm going, too. When we get back from England, we'll figure out whither we go next."

"Where we're going next," he murmured, "is to the closest available cottage."

It wasn't the honeymoon suite.

There was no freestanding glass-and-brass shower stall in the loft bathroom. The stone fireplace wasn't quite as massive as the one that had warmed them before.

But the Pines's management had provided a bottle of champagne with a dusty label that made Pete's brows arch, and the bed was as wide and as sinfully inviting as the one they'd shared.

Abby lay awake long after the fire had dimmed to a glow and the little bit of champagne in the green bottle had gone flat. Pete's head was heavy on her breasts, and his breath was warm against her skin.

She smiled, knowing she was home.

Epilogue

Distracted by the excited chatter in the outer office, Lucy Falco glanced away from her busy computer screen.

She caught a glimpse of Tiffany's silver curls, nodding emphatically, and the flutter of a gray reservation form in her hand. Tucking a stray strand of her dark brown hair behind her ear, she rose and joined the travel agents clustered around the older woman.

"*And* I have them booked into a medieval manor house for an entire week," Tiffany told the assembled group, lifting a finely penciled brow. "It's only open to a select clientele. Veddy veddy posh, you know."

"Who do you have booked into a manor house?" Lucy asked, smiling at her subordinate's somewhat less than successful attempt at an English accent.

"Abby Davis. Or I guess I should say Abby O'Brian. She and her husband are leaving tomorrow for London. I had to scramble to get her reservation changed to the same flight he was booked on, I'll tell you. Then I had to track down some information on this manor house she wants to stay in on her honeymoon."

"What manor house?"

Tiffany handed Lucy the gray confirmation sheet. "It's called Stonecross Keep. It isn't on any of our regular tour listings. I had to fax our contacts in London for a description of the facilities and a price quote."

"After the disaster at the Pines, I'm surprised Abby trusts us to take care of her honeymoon arrangements," one of the other agents put in.

"The ice storm of the century was hardly the fault of Gulliver's Travels," Tiffany declared loftily. Then she abandoned her dignity and gave an earthy chuckle. "Besides, who needs heat or hot water on a honeymoon?"

Lucy's lips curved in a wry smile. "Not Abby and her husband, evidently. Did you read the description of this place? It has no central heat, no electricity except in the modernized kitchen wing, and 'plumbing fixtures that give the visitor an appreciation of the medieval way of life.'"

"Oh, dear."

"You'd better give Abby a call and make sure she knows what she's getting into."

Tiffany's coppery earrings jangled as she nodded. "I will. And as soon as I finalize these arrangements, I'm going to start working the honeymoon package my bridge partner's niece wants me to put together for her. She's getting married a week before Christmas."

Lucy hid a smile as a fervent gleam came into Tiffany's pale blue eyes. After the disasters that had plagued their Halloween and Thanksgiving honeymoon packages, she could only hope the Christmas bride had a safe, relatively uneventful honeymoon.

* * * * *

The collection of the year!
NEW YORK TIMES BESTSELLING AUTHORS

Linda Lael Miller
Wild About Harry

Janet Dailey
Sweet Promise

Elizabeth Lowell
Reckless Love

Penny Jordan
Love's Choices

and featuring
Nora Roberts
The Calhoun Women

This special trade-size edition features four of the wildly
popular titles in the Calhoun miniseries together in
one volume—a true collector's item!

Pick up these great authors and a chance to win
a weekend for two in New York City at the
Marriott Marquis Hotel on Broadway! We'll pay
for your flight, your hotel—even a Broadway show!

Available in December at your favorite retail outlet.

NEW YORK

MARQUIS

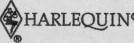

Take 4 bestselling love stories FREE

Plus get a FREE surprise gift!

Special Limited-time Offer

Mail to Silhouette Reader Service™

3010 Walden Avenue
P.O. Box 1867
Buffalo, N.Y. 14240-1867

YES! Please send me 4 free Silhouette Desire® novels and my free surprise gift. Then send me 6 brand-new novels every month, which I will receive months before they appear in bookstores. Bill me at the low price of $2.90 each plus 25¢ delivery and applicable sales tax, if any.* That's the complete price and a savings of over 10% off the cover prices—quite a bargain! I understand that accepting the books and gift places me under no obligation ever to buy any books. I can always return a shipment and cancel at any time. Even if I never buy another book from Silhouette, the 4 free books and the surprise gift are mine to keep forever.

225 BPA A3UU

Name	(PLEASE PRINT)	
Address	Apt. No.	
City	State	Zip

This offer is limited to one order per household and not valid to present Silhouette Desire® subscribers. *Terms and prices are subject to change without notice.
Sales tax applicable in N.Y.

UDES-696   ©1990 Harlequin Enterprises Limited

As seen on TV!
Free Gift Offer

With a Free Gift proof-of-purchase from any Silhouette® book, you can receive a beautiful cubic zirconia pendant.

This gorgeous marquise-shaped stone is a genuine cubic zirconia—accented by an 18" gold tone necklace.

(Approximate retail value $19.95)

Send for yours today...
compliments of 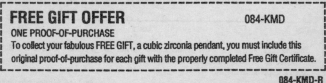 *Silhouette*®

To receive your free gift, a cubic zirconia pendant, send us one original proof-of-purchase, photocopies not accepted, from the back of any Silhouette Romance™, Silhouette Desire®, Silhouette Special Edition®, Silhouette Intimate Moments® or Silhouette Yours Truly™ title available in August, September, October, November and December at your favorite retail outlet, together with the Free Gift Certificate, plus a check or money order for $1.65 U.S./$2.15 CAN. (do not send cash) to cover postage and handling, payable to Silhouette Free Gift Offer. We will send you the specified gift. Allow 6 to 8 weeks for delivery. Offer good until December 31, 1996 or while quantities last. Offer valid in the U.S. and Canada only.

Free Gift Certificate

Name: _____

Address: _____

City: _____ State/Province: _____ Zip/Postal Code: _____

Mail this certificate, one proof-of-purchase and a check or money order for postage and handling to: SILHOUETTE FREE GIFT OFFER 1996. In the U.S.: 3010 Walden Avenue, P.O. Box 9077, Buffalo NY 14269-9077. In Canada: P.O. Box 613, Fort Erie, Ontario L2Z 5X3.

FREE GIFT OFFER   084-KMD
ONE PROOF-OF-PURCHASE
To collect your fabulous FREE GIFT, a cubic zirconia pendant, you must include this original proof-of-purchase for each gift with the properly completed Free Gift Certificate.

084-KMD-R

The spirit of the holidays...
The magic of romance...
They both come together in

HOLIDAY HONEYMOONS

You're invited as Merline Lovelace and Carole Buck—
two of your favorite authors from two of your favorite
lines—capture your hearts with five joyous love stories
celebrating the excitement that happens when you
combine holidays and weddings!

Beginning in October, watch for

HALLOWEEN HONEYMOON by Merline Lovelace
(Desire #1030, 10/96)

Thanksgiving—
WRONG BRIDE, RIGHT GROOM by Merline Lovelace
(Desire #1037, 11/96)

Christmas—
A BRIDE FOR SAINT NICK by Carole Buck
(Intimate Moments #752, 12/96)

New Year's Day—
RESOLVED TO (RE)MARRY by Carole Buck
(Desire #1049, 1/97)

Valentine's Day—
THE 14TH...AND FOREVER by Merline Lovelace
(Intimate Moments #764, 2/97)